I0626244

IT'S ALL GOOD

COOL JONES #1

BOBBY WEED

Copyright © 2014 The Good Word

All rights reserved. No part of this publication may be
reproduced or transmitted in any form or by any means,
electronic or mechanical, including photocopy, recording or any
information storage and retrieval system now known or to be
invented, without permission in writing from the publisher,
except by a reviewer who wishes to quote brief passages in
connection with a review written for inclusion in a magazine,
newspaper, broadcast or online service.

ISBN-13: 978-0-9919396-3-3
ISBN-10: 0991939638

THIS BOOK IS A WORK OF FICTION.
INCIDENTS, NAMES, CHARACTERS
AND PLACES ARE PRODUCTS OF THE
AUTHOR'S IMAGINATION AND USED
FICTITIOUSLY. RESEMBLANCES TO
ACTUAL INCIDENTS, NAMES,
CHARACTERS AND PLACES
ARE STRICTLY COINCIDENTAL.

THIS IS FOR THE BROTHERS AND
SISTERS OUT THERE WHO
BELIEVE IN THE POWER OF
LOVE

BOBBY WEED

PUBLISHED BY

THE GOOD WORD

1

On Monday morning, just after Christmas, I sat in my office, feeling bitchier than Scrooge. Even as a child, I hadn't liked Santa Claus any more than he'd liked me. A fat white dude up in the North Pole was going to bring me presents? Yeah, right. My bitchiness also came from going online and logging into my bank account. After entering my password, I saw that the bank had put five Ks into my account that didn't belong there.

"What the *fuck*?" I said aloud.

I liked banks even less than I liked Santa Claus, and the idea of stopping my current project so that I could call the bank and fix their mistake was enough to make me want to switch banks altogether. I minimized that window on my computer and went back to the preliminary report I had been writing about an insurance case a client had hired me to look into. Mercedes, the administrative assistant at Mutual of California, had called me to say that Lowell Mitchell, her boss, wanted that insurance file on his desk right away.

I wanted to help Mercedes and Lowell with that insurance stuff, but they would have to wait until I called my bank and told them about the five-grand Christmas gift they had given me by accident.

Once my bank issue was cleared up, I would get

back to that insurance thing. Norman Appliances, a company making air conditioners for other companies, had had a fire a couple of weeks earlier. Big fire. Nasty stuff. I had plenty of questions to ask about that blaze because it had totally gutted the warehouse. Arson? Maybe.

"Ronda Williams, Customer Care. How many I help you?"

"I just went online and found a ten-thousand-dollar deposit in my account that shouldn't be there," I said.

"May I have your name and account number?"

"Coolidge Jones," I said, giving her my account number slowly and clearly. Then she put me on hold while she pulled up my file. They kept me entertained with a Muzak Christmas carol.

Soon, Ronda Williams came back on the line. "Mister Jones, I'm not sure just what the problem is. I do see that there was a deposit in your account for ten thousand dollars on December nineteenth."

"Well, I didn't make that deposit. I do my banking online or in person. I don't want the money if it's not mine," I lied, "and I don't like the idea that someone else has access to my account. What do we do now?"

"We can track down the deposit slip," she said.

"Let's do it."

She said she would call me back when she knew something more. I thanked her and hung up. As a private investigator, I saw my share every day of people hacking and being hacked; it freaked me out that I personally might be the victim of that bullshit.

I went back to working on that fire claim, wondering what had happened out there at that Norman warehouse. The file had arrived at my office on the afternoon of December 23. I had agreed to have a quick drink with Emma Hendrix, my landlady, who was flying out to Philly to spend the holidays with her family. They're all old and so is she, and she doesn't know how much longer these holiday get-togethers will happen, so she cherishes them all. I promised to drive her out to the airport.

I had been sitting in my office that afternoon, finishing up some computer shit. Needing to stretch, I went to my huge window and stood looking out at the Pacific Ocean from the thirty-first floor. I live and work in San Francisco, California, the place I've called home for most of my life. I joined the Army and went overseas, then became an officer of the San Francisco Police Department. Now I'm a private investigator. Winter here means a little more fog and wind. We've had about one snow that I can remember, and it lasted for about fifteen minutes.

As a Christmas-basher, I laughed at San Francisco's half-assed efforts at decorating for the holidays. Some tinsel and boughs here and there, but nothing else. I guess it's hard to feel all Christmassy when people are walking along in Levi's jackets instead of parkas. Some Sally Ann volunteers sang carols and the stores were packed with shoppers, but life would return to normal soon enough.

My friends, and everyone else who knows me, will say that I am happy to be single. I am a childless man, a survivor of two divorces. I have no family ties to brag (or complain) about. As a private detective, I enjoy my job ninety percent of the time. Sometimes I work eighteen hours a day on a case or go on the road to find the bad guy, and other times I lock myself up in my minuscule apartment and read until I fall asleep.

When the Yuletide season arrives, though, and everywhere I look and listen it's family, family, family, I know I could throw myself a huge pity party if I let myself sink that low. Thanksgiving had been fun because Emma Hendrix had me and a few other of her friends for dinner, and I listened and laughed as they traded stories about their lives. I came away feeling it was too bad that I was thirty-five instead of seventy-five and could have had those adventures with them.

But Emma was about to fly away, and even Orlanda, who ran the bar where I often ate, was closing her business until after the New Year. Orlanda, tall, broad-hipped, bossy and brassy and sassy, wasn't my favorite person in the whole world, so I could easily survive a couple of weeks without her. But her closed tavern just sort of reminded me that I had nobody out there who had invited me for Christmas dinner and I would have to find someplace to eat that day, or go grocery shopping and put some shit away in my refrigerator so I'd have something to chow down on.

Anyway, after standing at the window and spacing out for a few minutes, I checked the clock and decided it was Miller Time. I put on my jacket and switched on my answering machine. As I started to think about what to have for lunch, Mercedes Jackson, the assistant from Mutual of Northern California next door, came in. After retiring from the San Francisco police, I had worked for Mutual on a full-time basis, mainly doing investigations on fire and wrongful-death claims. They must have liked my work, and I have to admit that I was a badass for them, because now we have this barter thing that works just fine for me: I am on call for them, and they compensate me with the use of some of their very expensive office space.

"Cool, I was afraid you'd gone," she said, handing me a file.

"What's this?" I hated being given work to do just as I was about to go home or out to eat.

"Lowell said to give it to you."

I looked inside and found a blank form. "Fire scene investigation," I muttered. "Guess they want me to do it. Haven't done one of these in months." I glanced at Mercedes. "Did Lowell really say give it to me? He's a boss. Bosses usually don't screw around with these minor things."

Mercedes smiled, blushing. "Lowell didn't actually say, 'Give it to Cool.' He gave it to Vince, and *he* said to give it to you."

I looked at the documents and said, "This thing is three days old. How come I'm getting it only now?"

"My bad." Mercedes blushed and smiled some more. "I have clutter all over my desk, and it kind of got lost."

Mercedes, pushing thirty, is one of the flakiest chicks I have ever met. I turned around and tossed the file on top of a few others stacked on my desk. "No big hurry," I said. "Later, girlfriend."

She pointed at that file. "Um, could you get on that *right now*?"

"Why?"

"Because Lowell *really* wants someone to get out there and check out that burned-out warehouse. Cicely was supposed to do it but she's on vacation and Lowell's, like, 'We need to get moving on this.'"

"Why?" I repeated.

"This claim is about a big warehouse fire in Oakland. You probably saw it on the news."

I shook my head.

"Well," she said, "the details are in the file. Like I said, Lowell wants some action immediately."

I resented her pushiness, or Lowell's, but opened the manila folder and had another look.

"Norman Appliances," I said, nodding.

"Do you know this company?" she asked.

"I used to know Allison Norman. We went to school together."

Mercedes bounced on her heels and beamed. "Awesome! I'll tell Lowell you'll be out there this afternoon."

"Chill on that. I have to take someone to the airport today. Tell Lowell, or Vince, or whoever, that I'll get on that file as soon as I can."

She nodded several times. "I hear ya, Cool. I'll leave a note with Lowell that you have the file and are gonna get busy with it. I better get back to my job. I got a zillion things to do. Let me know when you have the thing done and I'll come by and pick it up."

"You will be the first to know."

She darted away. Maybe I scared her off.

Immediately I called Norman Appliances and made an appointment to see Lloyd Norman, the president, at nine the next morning.

I didn't know that company presidents worked on Christmas Eve Day.

I checked the time. Close to four in the afternoon. I put the file into my knapsack, locked my office and walked home.

During out little two-person Christmas party, Emma gave me a Wil Haygood book and I gave her a Ray Charles CD. We sat in her kitchen, eating goodies and drinking champagne.

She looked at her plane ticket for the longest time, smiling. "Sure wish you'd come with me," she said as, in the background, Ray Charles sang about Jaw-juh. "Not too late, you know. I don't guess the flight to Philly is gonna be more than half full. Also, I don't like the idea of you bein' here all by yourself. It's not right."

I shrugged. "Wish I could, but Mutual just gave some work that'll keep me busy for a while. You just go to Philly, take some iPhone images and show them to me when you get back."

"What about Christmas Day? What you gonna do for turkey dinner?"

"Emma, quit worrying. I'll be fine." I would probably eat a day-old submarine sandwich and read a book all day, but she didn't need to know that.

She looked at the time. "Gettin' late. Maybe we should go now. The airport might be crowded." Her departure time was seven o'clock, an hour and a half, and the trip to the airport would take maybe half an hour, but I said, "Yeah, let's go." Emma, arguably the friendliest person I had ever known, would just get there early and find someone to talk to. For her, going to the bus station or airport and making small talk with strangers was part of the fun of traveling.

I put on my jacket and loaded Emma and her suitcase into my Ford. The roads were fairly clear and the drive brief.

By about six o'clock, I was back home feeling a heaviness in my chest. I've never liked saying goodbye to people I consider my friends and I hate it when they get to go someplace but I have to stay home. The sky started getting dark and the air had a wintry nip that I found oddly comforting. I let myself back into my microloft apartment and turned on the light. My building is in a neighborhood known officially as the Tenderloin; in other words, skid row. A few years back, some Hong Kong developer bought this building, at the time a flophouse called the Eleanor Hotel, and converted it into the Eleanor Apartments. Some might say it's not such an improvement. For only a thousand dollars per month, I get two-hundred ninety square feet of living space, a pull-down bed, a big color TV that is bolted into the wall and a bathroom so small that I can practically shit and shower at the same time. Since I own very few things, I have more storage space than I need.

Usually I look around my puny place and feel good about making do in such a modest way—"less is more," as the saying goes—but after dropping off Emma I felt depressed and lonely being back home, and a little voice inside my head said, *Maybe more is more.* I turned on the TV and saw nothing but Christmas shows. It reminded me of the choices I had made and the things I was missing. The man who has a family may wish he was single and carefree again; the man who has chosen the single life may watch Christmas shows and wish he had the comfort of a family. I turned off the TV.

Sitting on my pull-down bed, I felt hungry. In my refrigerator I took out a meatloaf-and-potatoes frozen dinner. I microwaved it and washed it down with a

King Cobra.

Looking out the window, I smiled again at the fact that the street I lived on, Turk, was still as much skid row as gentrified. On Turk Street, Christmas didn't actually exist for the poor people; and those gainfully employed folks who lived in the Tenderloin because it was half the price of other neighborhoods…they had gone home for a conventional Christmas with their families.

My parents were killed when I was a kid, and ever since then I hadn't gone for more than an hour without thinking of them. But I pushed them out of my mind and worked hard at thinking of nothing at all.

The clock said seven o'clock. I knew I would have a long, lonely couple of weeks.

IT'S ALL GOOD

2

The next morning was Christmas Eve day. I woke up, jogged three miles through downtown, showered, shaved, got dressed, had brekkie and was on the road towards Oakland before nine. I'd read through the file and still couldn't figure out what the big hurry was. Then I'd read everything I could find on my iPad. I learned that the warehouse was gutted, yes, but no one seemed to think arson was the cause—no investigations, no speculation that someone had torched the fucker. Those who knew about this fire said that an electrical malfunction had shorted out the sprinklers, and the warehouse had been full of paper products that burned instantly.

I frowned as I drank my coffee. I'd read a hundred of these things over the years. Shit happens, buildings burn, owner gets insurance check. If you're lucky, nobody is hurt or killed. Who why was Mutual bugging me about this one?

Maybe, I thought, there's something going on here, some devious, serious shit, that nobody is telling me about. Lowell, or maybe Vince, is under pressure from Norman Appliances to settle this claim in a hurry because they're afraid that if we look too closely, we'll see something that Norman Appliances doesn't want us to see.

Lowell and Vince are both ass-kissers when it comes to dealing with clients. Lowell is the boss, so he leans on Vince, who's having problems with his old lady and is eager to have Lowell like him and promote him. Vince is probably the one freaking out about this claim, and he's freaking out because Lowell's freaking out.

Oakland is where many San Francisco workers live, a place providing relatively affordable homes. While construction of homes in San Francisco is a hassle requiring City Hall's approval, Oakland's construction seems to be whatever its residents want it to be. To me, it's mostly ugly, full of crackheads and drive-by shootings, and I grew up making fun of Oakland and its people, even though I knew I was no better than they were.

The southern tip of Oakland was the location of Norman Appliances, with a few other businesses nearby. The city still had a reputation as a place of heavy industry, although those businesses had been sent to China and India years earlier.

I found Norman Appliances' business offices and pulled into the parking lot. Its burned-out warehouse sat a quarter-mile away. I would check it out right after my appointment with Lloyd Norman.

Their reception area was small, plain and functional, with a big poster on one wall advertising the N/A AC300, the air-conditioning unit used by countless companies all over the world. The poster included a bunch of facts about the air conditioner. It bored me shitless, but I did admire success, and Norman Appliances had been globally popular for decades.

The receptionist hurried in with a tall Styrofoam cup and a breakfast sandwich. His name tag said CLAY and his blondish hair looked spiky.

"Sorry! Hi! May I help you?" Clay asked. He was emaciated, his complexion scarred from childhood acne.

"I'm Coolidge Jones from Mutual of Northern California. I'm here to see Lloyd Norman at nine."

He gave me a big, embarrassed smile. "Is this about…arson?"

I smiled back. "Don't know if it's arson. I'm here to check out the fire claim."

"Well," Clay said, looking around the room, "Mister Norman isn't here yet, but he should be in soon. Want a cup of coffee?"

"I'm fine, thanks." I took the one available seat and grabbed a brochure on why the N/A AC300 was such a superior machine. I envied, and pitied, the kinds of people who had master's degrees in engineering and built things like air conditioners. What boring motherfuckers they must be.

Looking to my right, I could see some of the office staff at work. They seemed busy but gloomy and quiet. Maybe their business didn't make them have fun and bond with each other the way we did at Mutual.

They had put up a Christmas tree and trimmed it some, but nothing else. They were working on Christmas Eve, and maybe that pissed them off. I had read that the company grossed fifteen million dollars last year, and presumably everyone there made decent coin, so they should have had something to smile about.

Clay devoured his breakfast sandwich with much noise. "Sorry," he said after a big swallow. "I'm very hungry."

"Do they make you eat at your desk?"

"'Fraid so."

Behind him was a wall collage of employees and family members.

"Mind if I have a peek at that collage?" I asked.

"Be my guest," he said.

Some of the pictures were of Clay, who looked older than he was. I guessed he was just old enough to drink and had gone to work there just out of high school. In another picture, some guys in company uniforms lean against an air conditioner, hands in pockets, smiling as if at a dirty joke. The founder of the company, Guy Norman, had dropped dead in his office a couple of years earlier, and his employees probably still missed him.

At the center of the collage, Guy and his wife sat in a fancy photo, surrounded by their children. I had never met Lloyd, but I knew Allison from school. Ophelia, a bit older than Allison, had gone to school at San Francisco High but dropped out or flunked out, and her family had sent her to some boarding school where she couldn't run away. the Normans' oldest child, Edina, must be pushing forty. I'd heard she married some rich geek and moved to Europe. The youngest child, Brynne, had a Ph.D. in fucking up. She'd gone to New York City and Los Angeles to be an actor or musician or something. I knew about Brynne because she knew my second ex, Aja, herself a musician. I didn't know much about Lloyd but had a feeling that would change soon enough.

Lloyd apparently cared very little about things such

as punctuality and good manners. He arrived at nine-thirty, and Clay introduced us. "Coolidge," he said, "I have a quick phone call to make. I'll be right back." Half an hour later, he reappeared, his suit coat off, tie loosened and shirt halfway sweated through. He said, "OK, that's done. Sorry for the delay."

We went into his office and he collapsed into his reclining swivel chair, as if at the very end of a very tiring day. His thinning brown hair was already glistening with perspiration and his eyes seemed to have a nervous twitch. I figured he was lying about that phone call he'd needed to make. Lloyd Norman was the boss now, and probably jerked people around because he knew he was an important guy who could get away with it.

He sighed, swiveling a bit in his chair. "Now, what's on your mind?"

"You have filed a claim for a recent file loss," I said.

He brightened up, or got really defensive. I couldn't tell which. "Right—and I hope you're not going to give me a hard time with this, because my claim is totally legitimate."

I gave him a diplomatic little nod, even though a big red sign saying FRAUD ALERT was now flashing in my mind's eye. Every fraudster I had ever met—and I had met more than my share—had said something just like that. I withdrew my little voice recorder and placed it on his desk.

"Mutual of Northern California insists that I record this conversation," I said, switching on my tiny machine.

"I understand."

"The time is…" I said, looking at my recorder. I

said my name, his name, his company, why we were in his office. "Do I have your permission to record this conversation?"

"Yes," he said, rolling his eyes.

I studied the file for a moment. "Would you tell me the specific circumstances of the fire at Norman Appliances' warehouse, address eight-oh-nine King Avenue, on December nineteen?"

He stopped swiveling, puckered his lips and stared at the floor. "I think…I was out of town. all I know is what I've been told." Just then, his phone rang and he answered it. "Problem? This is a bad time. I'm in a meeting. OK, I'm on my way." To me, he said, "Excuse me—I'm needed elsewhere." He pulled himself up and hustled out of his office.

I turned off my voice recorder and thought for a few minutes about the man I had just met. He needed to join the Hair Club for Men and Jenny Craig. He also needed to spend a few bucks at Brooks Brothers and get the suits a CEO should wear instead of that gabardine shit he had on. Finally, he needed to get a job that didn't stress him out quite so much. The man was too damn young to be dying of old age.

After waiting for ten or fifteen minutes, I got up and went to the door. No Lloyd anywhere. Weird; I wasn't some dumbass salesman he could just blow off. I was an insurance investigator and he had a burned-to-shit warehouse. If he wanted the insurance bucks, he would have to go through me. I couldn't see Lloyd or Clay. I walked around a little and saw someone who looked much like Edina, but maybe it wasn't her. I looked at another woman and she looked up at me. Her desk nameplate said she was Davida Avalon, the company's office manager. She looked like many other office managers I had met—petite and humorless, a middle-aged woman with short black hair and tortoiseshell glasses. She tilted her head, as if to say, *What the fuck do* you *want?*

I smiled. "I was just starting a meeting with Lloyd Norman, but he excused himself nearly half an hour ago. Any idea where he went?"

"He's left the facility."

I frowned. "Gone? What do you mean?"

She shrugged. "Just what I said."

"When's he comin' back?"

"You would have to ask *him* that."

"Ahem," came a voice from behind me.

I turned around and saw a black-haired man standing there. "Davida, is this gentleman being looked after properly?"

"Oh, sure, Cody," said Davida, her attitude backing way off. "Sir," she said to me, "this is Cody Terryman, the company's vice president." Then, "Cody, this gentleman had an appointment with Lloyd, but he left before they got started."

"I'm Lloyd's brother-in-law," Cody said, shaking my hand.

"Coolidge Jones, Mutual of Northern California," I said.

Cody was a big man, tall and broad across, with a strong handshake and a dark, hard stare. If Lloyd was the wuss he seemed to be, Cody was the resident tough guy. Maybe Cody ran things while Lloyd acted like the boss. I wondered which Norman sister Cody had married.

"If Lloyd isn't here, maybe I can help you," he said.

I ran it down for him: the fire, the file, the

disappearing act Lloyd had done as soon as I turned on my iPhone's voice recorder.

"Let's go out to the warehouse," he said. "What's left of it, anyway. I assume you're going to need to see it as part of your job."

I nodded. "Is anyone else out here authorized to tell me what I need to know?"

Cody and Davida shot a very quick look at each other.

"Maybe," Cody said, "it would be better if you dealt with Lloyd after all. I have his cell number. I'll try to get him back here." He walked away.

I stood in the doorway for a few minutes, staring at Davida as she stared at her iPad. Then I moseyed on over a few doors and listened in as some engineer dudes rapped.

"Maybe my math is bad," one guy said, "but I kind of doubt that."

"If your math is bad," another guy said, "the machine will explode and good men will die like dogs."

They laughed.

"I have been asked, many times, and I'm not sure what the answer is…How would we be able to produce colder air in the smaller units that run at fifty revolutions per second?"

"How big is the motor for the smaller unit?"

"Twenty-five cubic centimeters."

"Ouch!"

"There is a reason that we make big air conditioners and small air conditioners. You're wanting to put big power into a little machine, and that ain't gonna happen."

I shook my head and ignored them. Engineers

were just too fucking boring.

Ten minutes or so later, Cody Terryman came back, shaking his head and shrugging.

"Beats the hell out of me," he said. "Lloyd says he's out checking on an emergency answers and I can't find Clay, either."

"I'll get my iPhone. It's in my knapsack."

Cody followed me into Lloyd's office. I put my iPhone into my pocket and left my knapsack where it was.

Together we walked through the offices, one of the bosses and the menacing-looking black man— me—who was there nosing around about that awful fire they'd had.

Their assembly work happened in a chilly, spacious area at the back. A place of metal and concrete where no fire would ever damage anything.

We walked fast, and stopped only once, so that Cody could introduce me to someone.

"This here's Sal Johnson, a chemical engineer who does consulting for us. He's been with us forever. If you have any questions about how we make air conditioners, he's your man."

"I'll remember that," I said as Cody kept moving.

I caught up with him as we left the place through a huge rolling steel door for shipping and receiving.

"Cody," I said, "which of the Norman girls is your wife? I went to school with Allison."

He grinned. "Ally's a great gal. I'm married to Ophelia. Your name again?"

"Coolidge Jones. Folks call me Cool."

He looked me up and down. "You ever play football, Cool? You're big enough."

"Nope. I've always worked out. Been in the Army,

was a San Francisco cop for a while. Now I'm a private eye."

We stopped talking as the blackened remains of what had been the warehouse came into view.

3

I spent close to three hours inspecting the fire scene. Cody and I grimaced at the stink of soot, and I felt surprised by how the outside of the building, although black from the fire, was still standing. The inside looked like something out of a horror movie: the second story had imploded onto the ground floor, and everywhere I looked was pure destruction.

"Windows are gone," Cody had said. "Maybe I should just kick in the front door. If I blow on it, the thing will probably collapse."

"No, use your keys," I said. "I'll need to take pictures, and I want this place as intact as possible."

When it became clear that I would be there for quite a little while, Cody said he would meet me back at the office.

"It's Christmas Eve," he said. "We're closing early, and I have some things I need to do." He added, "If you get done soon enough, come by for punch and cookies."

I nodded and muttered something, already lost in

my job. I had taken out my pencil, sketch pad, measuring tape and other tools. I looked all around, figuring out where to start.

I walked around the building, noting which parts of the structure had been burned worst. Had the windows been broken? It didn't look that way. Nobody had mentioned if a salvage crew was on its way, and since arson seemed unlikely, I didn't think Mutual had any reason to make the salvage boys wait.

Was Lloyd Norman secretly going broke? Had he paid someone to torch his warehouse so he could get some fast cash? I couldn't answer those questions just now, but on Monday morning, I would do a thorough background check on him and find out what kind of bucks he had and how much he owned and to whom.

I would do all of that because it was part of my job. I didn't think it was necessary because the fire chief had already said in his report that it wasn't arson.

Since this was the only chance I had to check out the warehouse by myself, without any well-intentioned fools standing over my shoulder bugging me, I took out my iPhone and started taking pictures. Most of the fire damage was near the electrical switches were—no surprise there. These blazes usually happened because electrical systems, for whatever reason, shorted out. As a cop, I had gone through many fire scenes, and the firefighters had taught me that fire travels upwards, eating up everything it can; while it's burning something, it starts traveling horizontally, and then it starts moving vertically again.

Anyway, I moved around inside the warehouse, looking at everything while touching nothing. I drew sketches and again winced at the reek that all fire scenes have. I could still smell my first fires from my days on the SFPD. In my nightmares I could also see the "crispy critters"—charred bodies. Fires were smelly things, and ugly things, too. This warehouse was full of burned objects that once had been something but now were nothing, and I wanted to know what they had been. I'd told Lloyd Norman on the phone that I wanted to see his inventory sheets, so I could tell what kind of weird burned shit I was smelling. I definitely wanted to sit down with him and ask lots of questions before seeing the warehouse, but he'd run off, so now I was on my own. As a private investigator, I knew that people saw me as being an authority figure, but that didn't stop them from fucking off when I started asking them questions they didn't want to answer. As a police officer, I'd seen people ran away from me, too. I hoped maybe Lloyd would return to the office for the Christmas party, and I would be able to bully him into an appointment for just after the holiday, but I had a feeling he would blow me off about that, too.

At two in the afternoon, I left the warehouse. I had ash all over my slacks and shoes, but I felt pretty sure I had done by job properly. Norman Appliances would need to get rebuilding estimates from a handful of contractors, submit those items to me, and I would turn them over to Mutual, along with my recommendation about payment of the claim. I would recommend half a million dollars for the payment claim but some extra money for the inventory loss.

They had started their party without me. The refreshments—a punch bowl, cold cuts, cheeses and crackers, some sort of cake—had been set up on someone's drafting table. The company had several dozen employees, and they got more cheerful as people kept doping the punch. I thought I heard some kind of Christmas music blaring through the public-address system.

I could not find Lloyd Norman, but I did locate Clay, who leaned in stoned merriment against one wall. Cody Terryman came up to me and said, "Let's go get your briefcase before someone steals it."

I nodded and we pushed past some people till we got into Lloyd's office, where they had set up another punch bowl. Lots of employees were in Lloyd's office, sitting on his furniture and laughing and pinching each other's ass. I had to do some looking to wind my briefcase, and discovered it between a couple of bookcases. I pulled it out and nodded goodbye to Cody.

"Why not stay for a drink?" he asked.

Normally, I didn't drink, and when I did, I did so with only with people I knew, and only when I could be pretty sure of what they handed me to drink. Standing there, I wasn't at all sure I liked those Norman Appliances people and I knew there was some shit in that punchbowl. But because I had absolutely, positively nowhere else to go, this time I said, "OK."

I stuffed my face with punch, cookies, cake, cheese and crackers, smiled back at a few women when they smiled at me, and looked away when a few white men looked at me as if they'd never seen a black man before. At about three o'clock, as things got louder and merrier and people started dancing, I got my knapsack and headed out the door.

"Mister Jones!" someone called out as I entered

the parking lot. "I have a present for you!"

I turned around and saw Clay. He had a Christmas present for me? I wasn't sure I wanted to receive whatever he had to give.

He held up a large manila envelope. "This is for you. Lloyd knows you want it. Happy holidays!"

He handed it to me and I looked inside. The inventory papers. Yes, that was a gift I wanted, but I still needed to sit down with him and ask him all those questions that he apparently didn't want to answer. "Thanks," I said to Clay. "I'll call later and reschedule my appointment with him."

"Sorry for the hassle," he said in a stoner's mellow voice. "Gotta run. I'm sure they've missed me." He hurried back to the laughter and music. Davida stood just outside, smoking a cigarette, staring at me as I inserted the manila envelope into my briefcase and got into my car.

When I returned to my office, I noticed that Mutual, like so many other businesses, had closed early on Christmas Eve. I unlocked my door, turned on the light, flipped the file onto my desk and called the fire chief to verify the information I had just gotten, but he, like any sane person, was at home on this day and wouldn't be available to deal with me until the day after Christmas.

By four o'clock, I was back at home, and stayed put. On Christmas Day, and the day after, I was alone, but not lonely. I drank lots of gourmet coffee, sat propped on my pull-down bed and read a few novels.

On the 27th, which was Monday, I went back to my office and, in a foul mood, sat at my desk and tried to do an early draft of that fire report.

My phone rang and I snatched it up, hoping it was the lady from the bank, telling me they had cleared up that stuff about the ten grand sitting in my account. But it wasn't.

"Cool? This is Mercedes. When will you have that fire file ready for me? My boss wants to see it."

"It'll be ready when it's ready."

"You know what? That sucks." Then, "I told Lowell that you wouldn't have everything done yet, but he's, like, 'I want to see what Coolidge has done so far.'"

"He wants it *now*? Why?"

"I don't know anything; I just work here. So, *please*?"

I sighed. "OK, come and get it."

I hated it when I had a fire claim to work on and the claimant seemed to be hiding something, the way Lloyd Norman did. I especially hated it when the Mutual boss, Lowell, copped an attitude and wanted to see what I had done so far. I felt he was questioning my competency. The first thing I had done that morning was to fill out a form for the state office that handles fraudulent insurance claims, to check on Lloyd Norman. Maybe I had come across some nasty business involving him and bells were ringing in my head. The computer check would take a week and a half, but when it did come in, I would have some answers.

When Mercedes came in for the file, I sat at my MacBook Pro and didn't look up. "I took images with my iPhone. I'll print them off in a few minutes."

"I'll tell Lowell," she said as she walked off.

She doesn't like me, I thought with a little smirk. She never has. Well, too fuckin' bad. I'm a lovable man.

On the form I was filling out, there was no section saying PLEASE INSERT YOUR PERSONAL OPINION OR GUT FEELING HERE, so I just typed in what I knew. When I was finished, I printed, signed and dated the document, then put it aside. I made little improvements on my warehouse sketch and put it into the file. Finally, I took out my iPhone and got ready to plug it into my computer to begin printing those images.

Then my phone rang.

"Coolidge? This is Vince. Please come see me in Lowell's office."

I gave him no backtalk, since he was the Mutual claims manager. "I'm just printing the images now."

"Just come in with what you have."

I said OK and gathered up the file. I locked my door and went to go see Mister King Shit.

The moment I entered the office, a little voice said, "Oh, fuck." I had known Lowell Mitchell for as long as I had worked for Mutual of Northern California, which was nearly a decade. He is nearly as retirement age now, and he has what's left of a Marines physique. His hair, about half gone, is brushed straight back, and his features have been softened with age. Lowell is smart, detail-oriented, conscientious and not at all chummy. His way of praising people is with silence, which is much better than yelling, which he will be happy to do if he catches someone fucking up. He has been married forever and has a large family, of whom he rarely speaks.

I got anxious as I entered the office, not because I had been called into Lowell's office by Vince to meet with both men, but because Vince had that certain "I've got you by the balls, nigger" expression I had seen before. Vince and I don't get along at all. In his early forties, Vince is a toady, a guy who's done well enough but always wants more. He is tall and fat, with a full head of graying hair and two or three chins hanging down. He wears Walmart clothes and waddles around the office. I dislike him because he's fat and lazy and thinks he's better than everyone else, especially me.

Lowell looked through the file. "Thank you, Vince."

"Excuse me?"

"I said, 'Thank you, Vince.'"

"You want me to leave?"

"Yes."

"But I thought—"

"Goodbye."

Vince shrugged and sauntered out the door. Lowell watched him close the door, then looked at the file some more. Finally, he said, "You want to tell me about this?"

I told him—about my trip to the warehouse, etcetera. I omitted the fact that Mercedes had forgotten about the file for a few days; if I'd told him that, he would have stuck his boot up her butt, and I didn't want that to happen. I told him that the pictures were ready to be printed. The estimates weren't in yet, but so far as I could tell, everything was routine. I wanted to add, *There's something in all of this that seems wrong and maybe illegal. I don't know what it is yet. You know what I mean?* But since I couldn't be more specific, I thought it best just to keep my mouth shut and tell him only what I knew.

What freaked me out was Lowell's puckered-mouth silence as I talked and he read the file. Lowell is a talker, a rat-tat-tat asker of questions, a man who, when he has the gist of your answer, cuts you right off with his next question. He simply doesn't look and listen, like he was doing right now with me.

"Lowell," I said, "what's goin' on?"

"Read this," he said, his voice icy. "It was inside the file."

He handed me a Mutual of Northern California memo slip, about the size of an index card, filled with Cicely's unmistakable handwriting. "'Cool,'" I read aloud, "this one looks bad—real bad. I apologize for being unable to give you more details, but the fire chief says it all in his report.'"

I shook my head. "This was *not* in the file. This is the first time I've seen it—"

"Oh? Wasn't the fire chief's report in there?"

"Absolutely. It was the first item I read."

Lowell let out a huge sigh. He handed me back the file. "Read what's there. The fire chief's report."

I nodded. "'Arson clearly suspected.'" I glowered at Lowell. "This is definitely *not* what the chief's report said."

I handed it back to Lowell.

"I got a phone call this morning accusing you of taking bribes," he said.

"That's bullshit. Who called?"

"We won't talk about that just yet."

"Well," I said, "when I was a cop, I always told people that if they were being accused of something serious, they should want to know who the accuser is."

He just sighed again.

"Lowell, at least tell me what that anonymous caller said."

"They said that you were observed accepting an envelope from someone at Norman Appliances on Christmas Eve."

I closed my eyes and saw Clay hurrying over to me with a manila envelope. "The kid who works there gave me an envelope, saying it was the inventory documents I needed to see."

"I don't know anything about inventory documents," Lowell said.

"I put them in that file."

He looked through the file and pulled out a few sheets of paper covered with promotional messages. His face was grim. "Are these 'inventory documents'?"

"No." I took a deep breath. "I made an appointment to go down to Oakland and see Lloyd Norman. I had plenty of questions. When I got down there, he made me wait for a long time. When he finally showed up, I turned on my iPhone and told him I needed to record everything. So he excused himself and beat it."

"So you didn't get your interview?"

"Nope. That's on the to-do list for today. Wanted to get the report done first."

"Is this the envelope that Clay gave you?"

I looked at it. On it, someone had scrawled, *Hope this will do for now. More later.*

"Dammit, Lowell," I said, "you don't think I'm taking bribes from these people, do you?"

"Coolidge," he replied, "I don't know what to think right now, and it really doesn't matter what *I* think. But I *do* think we better look into this thing."

"Well," I said, "if I did take cash from them, what would I do with it? Where would I put it?"

"There are a hundred places," he said.

"Am I a fool? Huh? Am I a fuckin' fool? If Lloyd Norman wanted to bribe me, he wouldn't do it by sticking cash into an envelope and writing a note on that envelope. This is the dumbest frame job I've ever seen!"

"Why would he do such a thing?" Lowell asked, as if I knew the answer and he wanted it explained to me.

I shrugged. "Maybe Lloyd Norman is in trouble with organized crime or something, and then I come over to his warehouse asking questions, and so I become part of his trouble. Shit, man, I don't fuckin' know. I got enough trouble of my own with my bank telling me I have ten thousand…"

"Ten thousand what?" Lowell asked, but I really didn't hear him. I broke out into a cold sweat, understanding now why my balance was higher than it should have been.

IT'S ALL GOOD

4

I packed my personal shit, which wasn't much, and loaded it into my car. I usually walked to work, but Mutual, because of the Norman Appliances issue, had told me to go home until they could "resolve" matters. So I had gone home, gotten into my car, driven it to Mutual's carport and gathered all my stuff. Mutual didn't say anything about wanting their keys back, and I wouldn't have returned them, anyway. I would be back. My gig as the house detective was too good to walk away from.

Now that I had some time to kill, I went slowly and carefully through what had happened. Everything was OK until I drove out to Norman Appliances and went to the warehouse while I left my knapsack in Lloyd Norman's office. I hate to admit it, since I'm a private eye and a former cop, but I sometimes leave my knapsack unattended, and I had the file in my knapsack, so Norman's people had access to it. I also keep my checkbook in there, so they could have used one of my deposit slips to put the ten thousand into my account.

I drove out to Norman Appliances, full of determination to ask many questions, get as many answers, and exit that place with someone's ass in my knapsack. They had gone to some trouble to make me look like a chump, but was Coolidge Jones going to let the bad guy get away with it? No fuckin' way! I had been a cop, and I had seen my share of people attempt insurance fraud and end up doing several years in the state pen because the insurance people and private investigators—like me—were smarter than the fraudsters.

Clay swallowed hard when I entered the reception area and marched up to him.

"May I help you?" he asked, swallowing hard.

"I'm gonna see Lloyd."

"Do you have an appointment?"

"I certainly do." I walked past him and opened Lloyd's office door. He was sitting at his desk with Sal Johnson, the chemical engineer I had met my last time out there. The two men were pointing at diagrams on the desk and talking over each other. Maybe they thought they had reinvented the air conditioner and were bragging to each other about all the money they were going to make.

"I want to talk to you," I said.

Lloyd nodded at Johnson, and Johnson took off. I leaned over Lloyd's desk and said, "Someone is tryin' to fuck us both up the ass. Problem is, we ain't gay, so this bad guy? He got to be got." I ran it down for him and watched his face turn from raspberry to vanilla to raspberry again.

He sat back and said, "Ugh. Unreal."

I sat down and said, "Last time I was here, what

was that emergency that made you run away from me so fast? I think if we had done that interview, you would have said something about arson, and I would have known that the fire department's report was a fake."

Lloyd nodded and took a moment before he spoke. "You may have thought that emergency was a fake, but the truth is, my housekeeper called to say that my ex, Anya, had shown up with two big men and a moving van, and they were in the process of cleaning me out. Divorce is a dirty thing."

"Tell me about it," I muttered.

"Don't think that she's involved in arson or in trying to destroy me financially. She wants me to stay alive and make money so that I can pay her thousands per month in alimony. Also, she's been out of state for most of this year."

"Can she prove that?"

"Anya is a cunt. If you were to meet her, you would think the only thing on her mind was which credit card to use while shopping at Neiman's."

"Well, *someone* wants to fuck you up," I told him.

"How do you know it's *me*? Maybe they're after *you*."

I shook my head. "I got this fire-investigation assignment by chance. When shit happens, and an investigation is necessary, they give the job to whoever is available. If the bad guy was after me, he would go after me directly. He wouldn't say, 'Hey, let's torch this warehouse because Coolidge Jones might be assigned to investigate it.'"

"I hear you."

"So, what else is going on in your life? Any enemies who swore they would get back at you?"

He looked around his office for several long moments while continuing to swivel in his chair, as if the words he wanted to say to me were written on his walls. Finally, he spoke. "One of my sisters moved back here from Europe earlier this year. I understand that she thinks the company could become more profitable if she was in charge."

"You mean Edina."

He frowned. "You know her?"

I shrugged. "We've met."

"Well, she has plans that don't include me."

"Would she set you up and try to get you busted so she could move in and take over?"

Another big sigh. "I better get my lawyer in on this," he said.

"Me too." I got up and left.

I didn't think that anyone had notified the District Attorney's office of this matter or filed any charges. A valid arrest warrant must show that a crime has been committed and that a reliable person has provided the information about the crime. All Lowell had for the moment was an anonymous phone call and a burned-out building. He would have to get busy, of course. If the accusation turned out to have merit, Mutual would need protection. If I knew Lowell, he would pick through my Mutual workload and try to find signs of misconduct. Then he would hire some private dick to check out Norman Appliances, Lloyd Norman, and even me. I smirked at the idea of receiving the same kind of enema I had given to so many others. Whoever checked me out would certainly as questions about that ten-thousand-dollar deposit into my checking account, and I had no idea what to say or do about that. The deposit itself looked bad for me, but if I took it out and put it somewhere else or hid it in my closet—well, that would look even worse.

I remember the remainder of that day in bits and pieces. I spoke to Kenny Longman, a criminal lawyer I had worked with a few times. A college wrestler years earlier at Oregon State University, Longman had gained some weight but still looked powerful enough to rip apart a copy of the Yellow Pages. He usually needs a haircut and his suits have trouble stretching across his massive torso.

Attorneys, like other people in authority, can sit there and matter-of-factly say things that will make a person break out into a cold sweat. Like doctors, who will tell us that we will be crippled in a year or dead in a month, lawyers will sit nice and comfy and tell us how likely we are to be sued for everything we have or thrown into prison where rapists are waiting to sodomize us. When I ran it all down for him, Longman said that in addition to alleged insurance fraud, Lloyd Norman and I could be named as conspirators. Plus, I could face charges of aiding and abetting arson after the fact.

"The district attorney could probably find some more charges to throw at you," he said.

"Shitfuck," I muttered.

"I'm just saying what the D.A. might do. You're damn lucky no one was killed or hurt in the blaze. Then we'd be talking about *serious* prison time."

"But I don't *know* any of these people!"

"It's up to you to prove that." Kenny's lips pursed, as if he'd just heard I had been locked up at Corcoran, with Charles Manson as my cellie.

After a few moments of disgusted ruminating, I said, "In my years as a cop, I kept seeing the law protect the bad guys. Now I'm being treated like the bad guy. You know what? We need Dirty Harry to come to town and blow the bad guys' heads clean off."

"You're exaggerating, Cool."

"So tell me what to do."

"Stay away from Lloyd Norman."

"Not sure I have that option right now. I still have a warehouse fire to investigate."

"I thought Lowell Mitchell suspended you and took that file away."

"Well, someone's trying to set me up, and I kinda wanna know who the bastard is," I told him.

"So do your investigating, but be very careful. Right now you may be looking at an insurance-fraud charge. If you're innocent, things will work themselves out and you will be exonerated. Just don't get yourself into even bigger trouble."

"Meaning…?"

"Don't go over to Norman Appliances and get carried away and beat Lloyd Norman into a coma."

"Oh."

At home, I went through my boxes of files and called Roberta Jonathan in the missing persons department of the San Francisco police. As a man, and a former cop and soldier, I always insist that I don't need anybody's help in any way. Plus, I told myself that this call to Roberta wasn't exactly a cry for help.

I had met Roberta early last year, when I was working on a case. We had gotten together a few times since then, including in her bed. She is a blonde woman with gray eyes, pushing forty, direct, motherly, comical, conflicted, a person who still thinks all people, deep down inside, are good. She has a husband named Cameron who doesn't know if he likes men or women, maybe both, and they have two little boys he sometimes kidnaps. We liked each other a lot from the moment we first shook hands and said hidy, but I told myself I was too smart to start getting it on with another man's old lady. Then, one foggy, windy evening, I was on my way home from a frustrating interview with some dude who refused to tell me the things I needed to hear, I bumped into Roberta and we went to a bar and started drinking. I got just buzzed enough to say OK when she pulled me up to dance to the Slayer shit they were playing on the sound system. We danced, talked, drank, etcetera. At some point that evening I became a slut. I let her take me home and go down on me.

We both acknowledged, sort of, that we were lonely and wanted to be together, at least for a while. We made, and kept, dates with each other, but only with hesitation and reluctance. We had been married and deeply injured by the people we loved, and both of us probably asked ourselves, *Why am I getting into this shit again?*

The risking, the tension, felt good. Also, I am black and she is white—I loved the freaked-out looks on white people's faces when they saw one of theirs with a big buck nigger like *me*, who was going to impale her on his big black cock.

I thought of her a dozen times each day and

smiled whenever her blonde face appeared in my mind's eye. At the same time, I felt a profound sadness. I have been married twice and had my heart broken more times than I want to think about. All the while, Roberta's old man was having fun jerking her around. He said she was spending "too much time with her new friend," meaning me, and she needed to spend more time with her family, meaning their children, while he went and did his own thing.

"Missing Persons. Sergeant Tavisora. May I help you?"

"Joni, this is Cool Jones. Is Roberta there?"

"Hey, Cool. No, she's not here. Gone to Tahoe with the family. Didn't she tell you?"

"Nope. Know when she's comin' back?"

"First of the year. Want to leave a message?"

"Yeah, tell her I've jumped off the Golden Gate Bridge." Click.

With nothing else to do, and no one available to talk to, I got real busy. The only way I could defend myself was through Allison Norman, but I hadn't seen her since he were kids in high school. I diddled around on the Internet to try finding Allison's phone number. I got Lloyd's. Her mother, Georgia, was listed, but no Allison, but that didn't mean anything. Plenty of people had unlisted numbers so the telemarketers couldn't reach them so easily. Allison didn't have a Twitter or Facebook account, either.

I called Georgia Norman. A woman answered. I told her who I was and that I wanted to contact Allison. Lots of times, I lied to people when I asked them for information; cops, lawyers and private dicks consider lying a very useful tool. But this time I told her the truth, if only because it seemed more convenient that way.

"Coolidge? This is Allison! It's been years! What have you been up to?" I've met all the Norman women, and they all sound alike to me. They sound elegant, eloquent and erudite. Thoroughly American yet hardly Californian. So many young people from the Golden State spoke like the airheaded beach kids on TV; Mom and Dad Norman must have admonished their girls, "Be better than those people who use profanity and slang."

"I was trying to contact you," I told her, "and now you're on the line. Must be my lucky day."

"Lloyd told me you were in Oakland the other day. You needed to interview him about that awful fire. Is there anything *I* can do for you?"

"I haven't had much success talking to your brother, so I'd like to sit down with you."

"How about lunch? I'm always eager to reconnect with old friends," she said.

We agreed to have lunch at Sam's in North Beach. My usual outfit consists of a leather jacket or tweed sports coat, an open-neck white shirt, Levi's and Reeboks. One thing I hated about being a cop was the uniform, especially that bulletproof vest and crotch cup. The gun belt, with the radio and handcuffs wasn't too much fun either. Try driving around with all that equipment on you, then getting out of the car and chasing the bad guy. My current "uniform," consisting of my own worn, faded clothing, suited me just fine. I also carried my 9-millimeter Glock polymer automatic pistol, in case I ran into some bad guys while doing my job.

IT'S ALL GOOD

5

San Francisco is a crowded city; it always has been and always will be. Too many people who live here insist on owning cars, and too many people from outside the city drive their cars here every day. I own a car, but it's a piece of shit, so I was OK with taking the bus when meeting Allison for lunch. Throughout North Beach, parking is as big a nightmare as it is everywhere else, and the cops are eager to write tickets. So I took the bus.

Allison sat in a booth, waiting for me. Sam's is not the sort of place tourists go to unless they already know how good the food is. It's decorated as an old-fashioned diner, with fake red-leather upholstery and servers who wear tuxedos. I went up to her and she looked up, smiling. She looked much as I remembered her: short blonde hair, pallid complexion, pale blue eyes, a trim figure that would have gone to fat if she let it. Attractive rather than pretty—someone who had entered middle age still looking good because there had always been someone to do her worrying for her. She and I had become friendly in high school, although not precisely friends; maybe she wanted to show off to her white friends how liberal she was by getting to know this forbidding-looking black boy. She wanted to say to them, *See? He's harmless. He's just like one of us, only darker and poorer.*

She jumped up to hug me, and she still had her kittenish quality, an endearing clumsiness, as if she still hadn't learned to make all her limbs work together at the same time. She'd gotten her teeth straightened years earlier; her smile was big, bright and genuine. Although her family had money—I knew she was a Norman as in Norman Appliances, but nobody at school made a big deal of it, least of all Allison herself—she didn't act stuck-up or nasty. Her sister Ophelia had impressed me as being aloof, or perhaps merely shy, and Edina seemed overpowering and domineering, Allison seemed comfortable and largely carefree. On the first day of school, we were permitted in homeroom to sit where we pleased, so I sat near the window and Allison plopped down next to me with a smile and a handshake. Nobody looked at us with a smirk, as if she had just taken a dare. We made small talk that morning and did so many times thereafter. She was neither a cheerleader nor an honor student and had no aspirations in that direction; I played football but had little else to brag about. Our friendship, such as it was, was sincere but doomed to be brief. I went to her home and met her family; they shook my hand and smiled at me as if I were a mangy, stray black cat (which perhaps I was). She met my auntie and I made clever excuses for why Allison couldn't see my home. While the Normans were consistently kind to Allison's colorful new male "friend," even I figured out before long that she was a Norman and I was not, and never could be, and I probably was happier in my own modest little black world.

Over time, our differences overwhelmed me and I became so mute and indifferent to her that she began sitting and chatting with another white girl. She seemed unhurt by my rejection of her, if it was that. She still smiled and waved at me. Allison Norman: Nice professional, professional nice.

"Coolidge," she said, "you're really staying in shape and looking good. I'm glad you retired from the police. This city gets more dangerous every day."

"You look just the way you did in high school."

"What an insult," she said, laughing. "I'm glad you're in a new line of work, but you sure looked handsome in that police uniform."

"I miss those police paychecks, too. Anyway, you and I lost touch for a while. I went online to find your phone number but couldn't. I didn't know what to think."

She nodded. "Well, here I am. It shouldn't surprise me that you were a cop. One of our teachers said to me, 'I've been a teacher for years now, and it always seems that the meanest students I've met, the worst troublemakers—the bullies and sadists—don't end up in prison, they end up on the police force.' Well, Cool, that was you: a big mean badass."

I chuckled. As an angry young misfit, I had become a "stoner," meaning that I hung out with the other tough kids along the stone wall that bordered the school's south end. "Do you remember Wong, the kid with the bad overbite? He got his teeth fixed and went to med school. Now he's an eye doctor. He makes megabucks."

Allison rolled her eyes. "I never would have thought he would amount to anything. What about that Mexican kid? Gomez? Any idea about him?"

"He's a liquor distributor down south. May be distributing some other things, too, that pay a lot better. But that's just a rumor. You had a friend named Carmen, right? She was always shoplifting even though she could afford to buy whatever she wanted."

Allison nodded. "Carmen Kurtz. She's in San Luis Obispo now, married to some well-off guy and still a klepto. Are you married?"

"Twice divorced."

"Any kids?"

I shook my head.

"Me neither," she said. "I really enjoy being around them but not enough to have my own." She laughed and rolled her eyes again. Maybe she was a lonely person, delighted to have lunch with an old acquaintance, and would be happy to hear whatever I had to say. Poor little rich girl.

"When," I asked her, "was the last time we saw each other?"

"On my sister Brynne's birthday party at the country club. You showed up with that Whitney Houston lookalike. Whatever became of her?"

"Her name was Aja. I married her, then divorced her. She was number two."

"Beautiful girl," Allison muttered.

"In many ways, she was. In others, not so much."

"You sure could pick them, Cool. Tell me about wife number one."

"I'm too sober right now."

Just then our server arrived with the bottle of wine Allison had ordered. She didn't bother to look at the label or sniff its cork. "Just pour it, Phil." The server did so with a smirk. Allison, with her proper walk and talk and fine manners; was also refreshingly free of pretension and she respected everyone's dignity. We ordered Sam's special, a hash of ground beef, spinach, eggs and whatnot, and the server disappeared.

I told her all about my interest in the Norman Appliances warehouse fire and the question of whether it was arson.

"Wow, Cool, that was an awful thing. I sure hope Lloyd hasn't done anything wrong."

"I hope so, too. What's the deal with him? Would he be the kind to commit arson or hire someone to do it for him?"

Allison didn't get indignant. She smiled. "If he did, I don't think he would go around telling everyone."

"Yeah. But does he have any enemies who would do him like that?"

"Maybe. The whole company, and our family, have had a very hard time adjusting to Dad's death. Brynne is a goof-off and Lloyd is much too bossy for his own good."

"Those two must have driven your father bananas."

She smiled. "That's one way of putting it. My dad was very strict. He had definite ideas about how to raise children, but I thought he was a poor parent. He was at work too often to establish himself as a strong presence at home. He thought he could raise his family the way he ran his company, but that never works. We weren't employees, we were kids. Lloyd and Brynne pretended to obey him but did their own things behind his back. Brynne still can't seem to run her own life properly."

"Where is she now?" I asked. "Los Angeles? New York?"

"For now, she's in New York. She goes back and forth between the coasts. She says she's still trying to 'find herself,' both musically and personally. She knows there's family money she has access to, so that helps her wander around and not commit herself to anything." She shook her head. "What a piece of work she is. She came out here for Thanksgiving and said she wanted to move to London or Rome for a while because they had some musical things going on that she could relate to. If she does that, she'll be back when her money runs out. I'm sure she'll never 'find herself.'"

"And Lloyd had his own issues growing up," I said.

She nodded. "Just different issues. Lloyd got into all kinds of crimes. He got busted a few times, and Daddy came to the rescue. Daddy went ballistic over that."

Our lunches arrived, steaming hot and smelling better than delicious. My nose started running and I suddenly realized how hungry I was. Allison grabbed her fork and shoveled the food into her mouth, eyes closed, teeth grinding, Adam's apple bobbing. She made funny little noises like those I had heard in porno movies.

"Any good?" I asked her, grinning.

She responded by making some more porno noises.

We ate and she moaned. With her meal half gone and tears streaming down her face, she wiped her eyes, nose and mouth. "Yummy," she murmured, taking a long sip of wine. She let out a big, unstifled belch and her face turned the brightest pink.

"So," she said, apparently guessing that I wanted her to talk some more, "over the past half-dozen years, Lloyd started getting more interested in Norman Appliances, and Dad was delighted, because he needed someone to take over when he retired. Norman Appliances was my father's life work, his real pride and joy. He loved us, too, of course, but in a different way. He couldn't control us. By the time Brynne was born, my dad had pretty much thrown up his arms and said, 'I can never retire. There's no one to inherit my business.'"

"What about Edina?"

"What about her? She's a girl. In Dad's mind, girls didn't run companies, or at least not *his* company."

I chuckled. "Ever hear of Meg Whitman? Or Oprah Winfrey? They've done all right."

"Sure, but Dad didn't care. He thought men run companies and women marry those men, have babies and spend money. Edina showed plenty of interest in Dad's company and even went to Caltech to study engineering. Dad thought she was more than smart, but not tough enough. He knew how brutal the business world could be. He said it got worse every day—at first he was just competing against other American companies, but then the Japanese and Chinese companies got into it. Building air conditioners is a big deal and many businesses want them. It takes a tough business leader to make sure they have the best product and the most enthusiastic sales force. So Dad just didn't picture Edina as being that person. So she got married and took off."

"How did he feel about that?"

"Oh, he said if she hadn't gotten married and taken off, he would have groomed her as his successor. He could be *such* a prick."

"She's back in town now, right?"

She nodded. "She's divorced now, and good riddance to him. I'm not sure why she married him in the first place."

"Lloyd says she's pretty hot to take over the business now," I said.

"Oh, I'm sure she is. But it's nothing she's ever talked to me about. We aren't tight. We never have been."

"How about Ophelia? Does she want to take over the company, too?"

Allison laughed. "Well, ever since Dad died, we've *all* looked at Norman Appliances and said, 'Our family's business has no leader now. Maybe *I* should try being the president. I mean, those air conditioners pretty much sell themselves, right?'"

"Ophelia is married to Cody Terryman, who works for the company," I said. "Maybe *he* wants the top job, too."

"Cody's a nice enough guy, and he's devoted to Ophelia, but he lacks charisma and, in a very real way, already thinks he is the boss of the company. Of course, when Lloyd is there, Cody is such a brownnoser. They call him 'Cody the toady.'"

"Ophelia is a lucky girl to have such a devoted husband," I said.

"Oh, sure. I think Cody had learned a lot about appliances from Dad and wanted to go off and form his own company, but Cody lacks the drive and tirelessness to be an entrepreneur. So he played it safe and stayed on the Norman Appliances payroll."

"How do Lloyd and Cody get along?"

"Well enough. They clash now and again, mainly because one of them is named Norman and the other one is not. Cody backs off and basically says, 'Yes, boss, whatever you say, boss.'"

"How about Sal Johnson?"

She smiled. "Super-nice guy. He's the son Dad always wanted. Sal would have inherited the company."

"You said that Lloyd did some illegal things. What happened?"

"He broke into the plant and stole things."

"For real?"

"Sure. In high school, he needed walking-around money for girls, cars and fun. So when he went up to Dad and said, 'Gimme, gimme, gimme,' Dad said no, and Lloyd helped himself to some of the stuff in the plant. He tried to fence the stuff, but the fence was an undercover cop."

"Ouch."

"Dad was *so* pissed about it! He wanted Lloyd to go to jail for it, but that didn't happen."

"Did Lloyd learn anything from that mistake?"

"Not really. He got busted some more times. Maybe he just got a thrill out of taking things that weren't his. After a while, Dad got so fed up that he had Lloyd sent to a boarding school."

We talked about other things for close to an hour. At around two o'clock, Allison checked her watch and said, "I've got to be going. I promised my mom I would take her shopping. There are some things at Gump's she wants to buy and I'm going to take her to Wilkes Bashford."

"Yeah, I have some things to do and people to see, including your mom."

She nodded. "You have our number. Give us a call and come by the house."

"Are you going to move back in there?"

"No, just for the time being. I've already bought a house but they're doing some renovations, so I'm keeping my mom company for the next month or two."

The check arrived, I reached for my wallet, but Allison said, "This one's on me. I feel my family is sort of responsible for this huge hassle you're having to deal with."

I put up my hands with a smile. "OK, you win." She gave me Edina's phone number and we walked out of Sam's. I followed her to her car and watched as she got in and drove off. Then I went to look for the bus stop, but decided to walk home because it was such a sunny day. From North Beach to the Tenderloin was not such a hard walk if you were in good shape.

I entered my apartment, pulled down my bed and switched on my MacBook Pro. I surfed around my favorite porn sites for hours and wondered if I had a problem.

6

On Tuesday morning, since I was sort of unemployed for the time being, I went to the gym at six o'clock, a time when few other people are there and I can use whichever machines I want to without waiting for someone to finish with them. All of the equipment is where it's supposed to be and the place doesn't reek of sweat and booty. People who exercise are weird: years ago, everyone got lots of exercise—they called it "manual labor"—but then some folks built machines that did all that hard work so we could chill. But all that chillin' has made us fat, weak and diabetic, so we pay good money to do that physical work in a gym. I do everything you can think of; that's why I'm buff. The others in the gym, if they don't know me, probably think I'm a boxer or a 49er.

As I went through my sets, I mulled over my current predicament. Not a bad piece of work as frame-ups went; their timing was terrific. I felt pretty sure that the phone call to Lowell had come from Davida Avalon; but who insisted that she call? She wouldn't have gotten involved in all this ugliness of her own volition. Someone had gotten access to the Norman Appliances file, but how did they know enough to make up that fake fire-department report? That must have been done by someone who knew the routine at Mutual. Insurance investigations usually happen in a well-established way; someone who was ignorant of how these things were done could not have been able to manipulate things this way. So who *did* the manipulating? Mercedes? Lowell? Vince? And *why* would they do such a thing?

I did bench presses and squats. I jog every day, and since I'm now well into my 30s, I have this fear of getting old and flabby, of losing my edge. Plus, I see my share of guys my age or younger who gave the attitude, *Fuck it, I'm going to get old and fat anyway, so why bother fighting it by exercising?* I got done a little after seven, so I went home to shit, shower and shave. I put on my jeans, tweed sports coat and white button-down shirt. Mercedes' workday started at nine, but many times I had seen her having breakfast at the coffee joint a few doors down. She would eat a bagel, drink a cup of coffee, joke with the server, tap on her iPad and space out.

When I arrived at eight, I could not find her. So I ordered breakfast and waited till she entered the restaurant. At eight--ten, Mercedes came bounding in dark slacks, a matching sweater and a pea coat. She stopped as soon as she saw me; I smiled and her eyes darted this way and that, as if she wanted to beat cheeks out of there. Instead, she slipped into an empty booth. I picked up my plate and slid in across from her.

"Good morning," I said.

"Please go," she muttered.

"Aw, that's not very nice."

The server came over and placed a bagel and coffee in front of her. As I ate, I fixed her with an unrelenting stare she could not escape. She looked every way but at me. And what did I see in her? I saw an ungainly woman with a tameless mop of hair, a broad forehead, blemished skin and uneven teeth. I wondered what the TV reality show makeover specialists could do with her. She was between boyfriends, and that didn't help her attitude much.

"I know you know about the pile of shit I'm in," I told her.

"I know."

"Know anything else?"

"I know that I didn't have anything to do with it."

"If that's true, then you can help me find out who's after me."

She sipped some coffee and leaned over towards me. "Lowell said not to speak to you. He would *shit* if he walked in here right now."

"Why doesn't he want you to speak to me?"

"Because he doesn't want you to know anything you don't already know."

I frowned so hard that my eyeballs hurt. "How come he doesn't want me getting any information?"

"I just can't talk about it."

"Well, then, *I'll* talk and *you'll* listen."

She nibbled at her bagel and sipped her coffee

while I kept talking, as if we were friends making small talk.

"Even though I work out of one of Mutual's offices, they sometimes work with other investigators, so one of them could have been sucked into this mess. But it just happened to be me this time. I bet Vince is enjoying all of this. He's never liked me and it really bugged him that Lowell and I had this barter arrangement that allowed me to use one of the company's offices. I'm pretty sure that Vince wanted to be offered that office space because of its good view. Anyway, I'm sure that Lloyd Norman is the real star of this show, but I don't exactly what his role is—yet. For now, I'm just gonna talk to all the people who may be able to give me information, then I'll figure out who the bad guy is." I paused and smiled. "You know what? I'm kind of enjoying this. I've never worked for Cool Jones before now. I hope he doesn't fire me."

I checked her out for a few long moments. She looked right at me, not down or away, which I took to mean that I had her undivided attention.

"Help me," I said.

"Why? You don't like me."

"You don't like me, either. But we can start liking each other. Now would be the ideal time." I added, "Vince is a douche bag. We hate him. We have that in common."

She nodded.

"Do you think Lowell had anything to do with this whole mess?" I asked her.

"No."

"Then who is trying to bring me down?"

In a low voice, she said, "Vince seems to be

spending *way* too much time around my desk."

"Tell me why."

"The day Cicely went on vacation? Lowell said to Vince, 'Spread her work around to the others.' Vince was, like, 'I'll give the Norman Appliances fire file to Coolidge Jones.'"

"Nice guy," I said.

"What bugs *me* is that Lowell got pissed because he thought *I* had let the Norman Appliances file sit on my desk for three days. I did not do that. Vince stuck that file into his briefcase and took it home with him. I asked him why and he just ignored me."

"Did you tell that to Lowell?"

"No."

"Why not?"

"Because Vince is my boss and I don't want to snitch him off."

I nodded. "So Vince took the file home with him, which included the fire department report, and he doctored it on his own time. Sound reasonable?"

She shrugged. "I guess."

"So…" I smiled and writhed a little in my seat, as if I had a deck of cards and wanted to deal and gamble. "How about if you check out his office while I go to his home while he's not around?"

"He's moved. He's not at his house anymore. He and Noelle are calling it quits."

"Big Vince is getting divorced, huh?"

"Yeah, finally. They've had issues for years. She's really shaking him down, from what I understand."

"Nice for her. Do you know where he's staying?"

"Down by the beach. Around Forty-fifth Avenue and Golden Gate Park, I think. I'll look through his office."

"I can get his address easily enough. Give me your home number and we'll get to work."

She gave me her number and I paid for her bagel and coffee. Now that we were friends, and in cahoots, we didn't want to be observed together. Just down the street was the downtown office of TSX, the credit agency that knows so much about so many. I wanted to have a confidential conversation with a friend who works there. Some time ago she wanted me to find out about some fast-talking dude who'd presented her with an investment opportunity that was too good to be true. After telling the cops about him, she'd taken out her checkbook to pay me. "Keep it," I told her. "I have a better idea." I have a great deal of respect for barter—I got my Mutual office that way and believe that both parties can benefit from a cashless transaction. Now I check out whichever new man wants to have dinner with her, and in return she slips me information I'm not supposed to have. Sometimes she would need a week to give me what I wanted, so on this trip, I asked her for whatever she had on Lloyd Norman. She promised to have something for me in a day or two; I asked her for something on Vince Stanich, too. Specific financial information on Norman Appliances was something I would need to get from someplace like Dun & Bradstreet. I could also get a shitload of information from Mutual of Northern California, which had done so much business with Norman Appliances when Lloyd Norman applied for coverage. I would have to ask Mercedes to log in on her computer and get into those sensitive files. It felt good to have her as a friend now after having her as an enemy or adversary for so long. A person can never have too many friends nor too few adversaries.

As I walked past the huge garage where Mutual people parked, I spotted Vince Stanich pulling in. We made the briefest eye contact before he looked away.

Back at my apartment, I began feeling claustrophobic. I had always taken my Mutual office for granted; I conducted nearly half of my business from behind my desk in the highrise, swiveling in my chair as I yakked away on the phone and stared at the screen of my MacBook Pro. I spent more than half of my time on the road, but it sure was nice to have that little office to go back to. I really started missing my office as soon as I lost it. That really sucked.

Since the time was just after ten in the morning, I knew I had to get busy. I turned on my MacBook Pro and started entering notes into it. Then I deleted some ancient files and made some invoices to send to clients who still owed me money. I hated every moment of it—what I *really* wanted to do was go out into the streets and bust some bad guys. I called Mercedes at Mutual and asked her for Vince's address. She gave it to me as she watched him walk down the hallway to the men's room.

I called his home number and got his answering machine. I changed into a generic sort of uniform—dark slacks with stripes down the sides, dark shirt, dark windbreaker with a patch on the left breast saying NORTHERN CALIFORNIA SERVICES. I topped it off with my shiny black SFPD shoes. Finally, I grabbed my iPad, lock picks and master keys. Looking in the mirror, I saw a big black man who had some sort of thankless city-services job. No one would question when he saw me entering Vince Stanich's apartment. I got into my car and drove out towards the beach, to violate a big fat white guy who had it coming.

7

The Monterey Apartments, Vince Stanich's new home, should have been called Majestic White Tower by the Beach. An obviously old building that had survived some earthquakes. I felt very lucky to find a nearby parking spot. I pulled in and got out. At the front door, I saw a black directory with names and suite numbers. I pressed several random numbers and was going to tell whoever answered that I was so-and-so with a municipal agency. My big black voice often worked well in such instances. Problem was, everyone was out—probably at work, slaving away to pay the huge rents at the Monterey Apartments.

The second problem was that all residents need to punch in a four-digit code to get in. I tried that, too, and failed. I had, however, noticed that the building had its own carport. So I got back into my car, turned on the engine and waited until a resident drove by and, with his handheld remote, clicked and waited for the gate to rise. When it did, I piggybacked him all the way past the gate. I saw him shoot a look into his rearview mirror, see my stern black face, and look away. Alarms did not sound; Dobermans and pit bulls did not charge out barking and clawing. The only security that fancy-ass place had were the locks, which I could easily pick now that I was in, and the residents, who were unlikely to hassle me.

I pulled into tone of the many vacant parking spaces and waited till the guy I had piggybacked got out of his Lexus and pressed the elevator door. He was a skinny, gray-haired white guy, probably a homosexual who shared his suite with his boyfriend. So the residents were gone for the day and building was occupied mostly by fancy gentlemen who liked expensive things. I knew a hundred desperadoes who could get past the Monterey's piss-poor security in two minutes and score the place in a few hours.

I took the stairs to Vince Stanich's suite, 642, and knocked on the door. Nobody answered. I waited for a few minutes and looked around to see if anyone might be on the sixth floor. Apparently I had the entire floor to myself.

The front door lock was an Apex. I took out a few of my picks and tried them, but the fucker wouldn't budge. I started to sweat and mutter some filthy words, hoping nobody could come by and wonder why this big black dude in some kind of uniform was dicking with the lock. If he was a locksmith, and he sure didn't seem to be one, he clearly had no idea what the hell he was doing. Finally, I used the right pick and the lock went *click*. I wiped trickle of sweat off my jowl and opened the door.

I love being where I'm not supposed to be. It's lots of fun. So is going online and seeing a bunch of shit I'm not supposed to see, or overhearing shit that was definitely *not* meant for my ears. I could understand why burglars broke into people's homes. The adrenalin rush is almost as good as making love. Going through that prick Vince Stanich's home was exhilarating.

I went through all the rooms, just to make sure I was alone. This building, like so many other old ones in San Francisco, had a master bedroom connected to the living room by a balcony, and the balcony had a ladder that led down to the street below. I could use that for a quick escape if someone came barging in during my visit.

The only thing that disgusted me more than my own stinks and messes was someone else's filth. I sneered at the sight of Vince's XXXL dirty clothing piled everywhere and stepped around it as if his shit-streaked skivvies and sweat-stained undershirts were mountains of steaming feces. As a man living alone, with no one to pick up after him, Vince had reverted to the slob he surely had been in his bachelor days. His bed was a box spring and mattress; his furniture consisted of rickety tables and chairs. His clean clothing, such as it was, sat half-folded in a corner. Next to his bed, a stationary bicycle sat unused. Why would a porker like him own something like that?

In a suitcase were checks and deposit slips, all bearing his name and account number. I also found a love letter, written by him, but not to his wife. He went on about her titties, vag and ass like a mediocre smut novelist, without saying much about her keen mind and beautiful soul. Her sexual prowess had him walking around with a boner that wouldn't go down, and after he had printed it out, he evidently felt he'd said too much or the wrong things—his redactions were many. I supposed their affair, or whatever it was, happened around Christmas Eve.

"Vinnie, you dirty dog," I said aloud with a little laugh.

He said something like he wanted to do her, and have her do him, but too much had been crossed out. There was very little of the tragic poet's eloquence in Vince, though much of his letter, with its clumsy begging and pleading, yearning and burning, made me nauseous. So had all the fast-food wrappers and empty beer cans in his kitchen. He had boxes, taped but unlabeled, stacked in one corner, and of course his suitcases. How long had he been separated?

I had met Noelle at a few Mutual office parties and written her off as another skinny, mousy blonde. I thought of her again as I picked through Vince's shit. The bitch had really cleaned him out. At work, Vince had ragged, to whomever would listen, about Noelle's spending sprees at Gump's and Neiman's and Wilkes Bashford, while she dressed her man in discount-store or big-and-fat threads. He liked it, in a way, that he could complain about her spending because it reminded us of how much he was earning. But now I knew that Noelle was not fucking around. She had married a man with money, no longer had any use for him, and cast him aside. Now he made do with a card table, aluminum chairs, a mattress and some dishes that he didn't need because he ate take-out meals and frozen dinners all the time. I got ready to depart, feeling I had now gotten to know Vince Stanich, a sad and lonely man.

I gathered up the papers I thought I might need and went back to my car using the stairs again. At home, I checked my answering machine.

"Hey, Cool? It's Allison. I spoke to my mother about this business with Lloyd and she would like to talk to you about it. Call me and we can take it from there. See ya."

I called her back, but her number was busy. I got out of my uniform and put on some normal clothes. I kept trying her number, and finally got through, but by then Allison's mother had gone for a nap. I agreed to drive up there for a cup of coffee at four.

Because I had some time to kill, I decided to take a drive up to the Presidio Gun Club and fire my nine-millimeter Glock for a while. I got into my old Taurus and drove up Turk Street, then turned right on Van Ness Avenue. The Presidio, originally a military facility—thus its name—is a large piece of beauty in the northwestern corner of the city, high above the bay so that the soldiers could see who and what might be coming in or going out. I live in a Tenderloin microloft, and I'm OK with that most of the time because it forces me to keep my personal possessions to a minimum, and I'm at home, usually, just to sleep or space out in front of the TV set. Also, I don't make enough money most months to move to a better neighborhood. If I were a rich retired cop like Joseph Wambaugh, I would move to the Presidio, an area filled with wooded areas, hills and scenic vistas. The sight of the Golden Gate Bridge always enthralls me; the sight of Tenderloin crack whores depresses me.

I reached the Presidio Gun Club, where I had often practiced shooting as a city cop. I looked around the parking lot and realized I was the only one there. I paid my fee and went inside.

"Got the place all to yourself, Cool," said the man.

"Just the way I like it," I lied as I got my goggles, gun and ammunition ready. I had always enjoyed the firing range with the other cops, mainly because I could outshoot most of them. I have always had excellent hand-eye coordination, so learning to fire a handgun came quickly and easily to me. My little Glock was hardly what I would have called the ideal firearm, but what the fuck.

I fired many rounds at my target from 25 yards away, most of my shots hitting my paper man in the heart. Beat *that*, Dirty Harry.

By just after three I felt exhausted and had run out of ammunition. I wasn't sure I had accomplished anything, but it was the highlight of my day thus far.

8

By three-fifty, I was pulling into the Normans' immaculate driveway in Sea Cliff, another of San Francisco's old-money neighborhoods where most of the houses had spectacular views of the bay. The world must really have bought lots more Norman air conditioners since I was Allison's friend; the family had a much more modest house back then. This place was a behemoth vision of white, with a large formal entrance and hardwood floors.

A big black woman greeted me, sort of, and motioned for me to follow her. She probably thought the lady of the house was going to interview me for a domestic job. After all, would a Norman really have someone like *me* over just to socialize?

"Wait here," she said as I took a seat in the morning room. The Normans' mansion impressed me until I started thinking about that feature I had read in *Architectural Digest* about novelist Danielle Steel's Washington Street mansion, with its 55 rooms, ballroom and enough space to park her dozen cars. I wondered how comfortable Steel felt as moved around in that place; did she scratch her ass and fart in front of the domestic help? Then I remembered reading that she had pretty much moved to Paris and made only occasional trips back here. She said she was happy to leave because San Franciscans dressed like slobs. Go figure people.

Soon Allison entered the room with her mother. Missus Norman, I guessed, was in her seventies but looked much older and used a walker. I flashed back on her as a handsome, sturdy, classy lady with a kind (or pitying) smile who was determined to forget, and make me forget, that I was a black boy who'd come a-callin', sort of, on her daughter. I had looked at her back then with the belief that she would never get old, since rich people seemed to be able to rise above such ordinary things as aging or being ugly.

"Nice to see you again, Coolidge," Missus Norman said now, peering at me as she gripped her walker so as not to fall on her face. I supposed that her husband's death had weakened her, especially since she now might have felt that she had the sole responsibility of being the head of the Norman family. Her hair was now a puff of cotton candy. Her turquoise dress probably cost more than I earned in a year.

Soon the maid brought in the tea cart laden with tea and faggot sandwiches—dainty little fuckers with their crusts removed. Still, they smelled and tasted great.

"You must be hungry," said Missus Norman with a smile as I stuffed a couple of yummy little faggot dainties into my mouth and slurped down some tea.

"Yes, ma'am," I replied.

"So am I," she said. "Food has always been one of my passions, and it always will be."

"Mine, too," said Allison, patting her stomach. "I should be a blimp by now, but I starve myself sometimes."

"You look the same to me," I said shrugging. "I mean that as a compliment."

She laughed. "I had a crooked nose, an acne problem, an overbite and I roll of flab around my middle that wouldn't go away. We had it all taken care of with rhinoplasty, orthodontia and dermatology."

"Well," I said, "it paid off."

We talked about our days in high school. Missus Norman reminded me that her husband and she came from humble beginnings. "After World War Two, my father and father-in-law knew each other and just wanted to make a decent living with machines or whatever. Neither of them had an entrepreneurial bent. But they knew from their time in the Army about heating and air-conditioning units and how popular they were. So they took what they knew and started Norman Appliances. We didn't think it would become big, thriving company, with business all over the world using our air conditioners. The company has survived for decades, and we have this big house, but I don't know that we're considered a 'society' family. We've never been invited to the hoity-toity social events. I don't think Guy was ever considered eligible for the Bohemian Club, but I'm sure he would have loved to join it. Did John Traina or Al Wilsey know of us? How about Dede Wilsey or Danielle Steel? Gordon and Ann Getty? I don't think any of those people had any use for us, and I've often wondered why."

"Don't feel too bad," I told her. "Those folks don't want to hang out with *me*, either."

We all laughed, and at five o'clock Allison left the room. Missus Norman leaned in towards me, her sociable manner now much more businesslike.

"Now, tell me about all this trouble with the fire and the insurance," she said.

I told her as much as I knew, and clearly Allison had already told her most of it, but she wanted to hear it from me, in my own words.

She pointed at me and said, "I want you to take me on as a new client and clean up this mess."

I shook my head. "No can do. Number one, my lawyers hate the idea of my coming out here and speaking to you. They especially want me to avoid Lloyd. I definitely can't accept work and salary from the Norman family. It already looks as if you people have been paying me off."

"I need to know who's making all this trouble for us," she said.

"I hear that," I told her. "The thing is, maybe the bad guy is one of the Normans. Not trying to offend you, but when some bad stuff happens, everyone is a potential suspect."

"Then we have to move on this right away and stop the 'bad stuff.' I don't like unethical, illegal business dealings, especially when they involve someone from outside the company. Please keep me informed."

I nodded.

"Tell me what I can do for you *right now*," she said.

"I want to know about Guy's will. How did he divide his estate? Who was supposed to run the company?"

The old woman's face hardened with resentment. "That was the only thing Guy and I argued about. He said, 'I'm leaving the company to Lloyd,' which I didn't necessarily think was a bad idea. Of all our children, Lloyd seemed to be the most qualified to run it once Guy was dead. But I believed that Guy should have given him the authority to go with the title. Guy said no. He just wouldn't give him absolute control of the company."

"I don't understand," I lied. "If he's the boss or president, doesn't the power go with it?"

She shook her head. "Did you know that in the very early days of Apple, Steve Jobs had the title of chairman? But for all practical purposes, Steve couldn't do much without getting the approval of the other bosses." She smiled. "When Apple was building their first plant, Steve had them install *our* air conditioners. He said to Guy, 'At least they let me be in charge of the air conditioners and heaters.'"

Her face hardened again. "Anyway, the title doesn't always mean very much. I said to Guy, 'Why give the boy the position without the power? Don't be a fool!' but Guy said, 'Absolutely, positively not!'" She shuddered and got a firmer grip on her walker.

"What was Guy's problem?"

"He was afraid that Lloyd would destroy the company. Frankly, Lloyd's judgment is sometimes quite poor. He's very impulsive, and he might say something like, 'The whole world is in love with Norman air conditioners, so this company is indestructible.' Well, I'm sorry, but this company is *not* indestructible. The world loves our appliances, but there's plenty of competition out there. The company grew because Guy really knew about air conditioners and what they could do, and couldn't do. Also, he had a businessman's understanding of how the market functions and how to get along with suppliers, distributors and customers. Lloyd really doesn't understand any of that and isn't terribly inclined to learn. He's quite a smartass and know-it-all. He has matured a little bit, I suppose, but in Guy's final years of running the company, Lloyd would get these awful ideas about how to run the company, and Guy would have to sit him down and straighten him out. But then Guy would come home and say, 'If I wasn't the boss and Lloyd had the say-so to do whatever he wanted, he would trash the company in fifteen minutes.'"

"Then why not find someone else to run the company? Ophelia, for instance."

"Are you kidding? Guy insisted that his successor be a man, and Lloyd was his only son."

"Edina also seemed like someone who wanted to run things."

"Yes, but then she ran off to Europe and seemed content to stay there forever."

"How did Guy divide the stock?"

"Lloyd got forty-eight percent, I have nine, our lawyer has three and the other kids have ten apiece."

"Why did he divide it so unevenly?"

"So that Lloyd would not have sufficient power to act alone. In order to gain a majority, he must persuade at least one of us that what he wants to do as company boss makes reasonably good sense. Mostly, he's free to put on his suit, go down there to his office, act important and pat himself on the back. The company pretty much runs itself."

"But if he got carried away, the rest of you could handcuff him."

"Oh, sure. We can outvote him and temporarily strip him of his powers. But it would sure drive him batty." She paused. "I won't live forever, and when I die, if I left three shares to Lloyd, that would give him a majority stake and he could run the company however he chose. If the others didn't like it, too bad for them."

"But for now, things are OK, so far as you can tell."

"As good as they can be considering Guy isn't here any longer. As I say, the company runs itself, and there's a young Norman out there reminding everyone that it's a family owned American business. We make good air conditioners and our reputation speaks for itself. Behind the scenes, we've got other Normans saying, 'If Lloyd can prove he's the man who can handle the job, fine. Otherwise, we'll keep looking over his shoulder to make sure he doesn't do anything terribly stupid.'"

I laughed. "Sounds like you're the matriarch of a soap-opera family."

She laughed, too. "If Lloyd thinks he can come to me with a bad business idea and I'll support him, he's an idiot, and I'll be happy to say so right to his face." She looked up at the clock on the wall. "Time for my swim. Doctor says I need to swim every day because I have two dozen medical conditions that will benefit from my swimming. One of the great things about this house is our swimming pool. It's quite a luxury to have your own pool in San Francisco. Want to join me? It's boring to swim alone, and we have some swimsuits here that will fit you."

I smiled. She probably thought I was smiling out of gratitude; in truth, I was smiling at the looks on her neighbors' faces if they saw big black Cool Jones swimming in the Normans' pool with Missus Norman.

"Thanks very much for having me over," I said.

"You're very welcome. I'll see to it that my whole family helps you as much as possible."

"That would be fine. I know the way out."

As I crossed the foyer, the front door opened and Edina entered. I hadn't seen her in many years, but I recognized her right away. I remembered when I was seventeen and she close to a decade older, and I thought she was *so* mature and sophisticated. She still had quite a presence, in her tight jeans and gray sweatshirt. Edina was still tall and emaciated, all eyes and cheekbones and lips. Her long hair was very black, her eyes very blue. Her skin was very white but her lips were naturally deep pink. She had gone to Europe to model just after high school, and she still walked like she was squeezing a dime between her ass cheeks. I had always wondered why the rich Americans were always hurrying off to another continent. She had studied for a couple of years at Caltech, then dropped out to dabble in photography, dance, fashion design and freelance journalism. She could do this, and maybe fail at it, without feeling badly because she had no pressing need of a paycheck. She had been married to some guy who, last I heard, was running around with one of Donald Trump's ex-wives.

She frowned a little when she saw me, and first she probably thought I was there to check the pool. Then she gave me one of her icy little smiles.

"Hello, Coolidge. Come with me. We have some things to talk about."

I nodded and followed her upstairs. That woman lacked all the charm that Allison had. I hoped she would answer my questions with total honesty and plenty of detail, but I doubted it. She seemed like the kind of person who liked jerking others around.

I looked at her as she climbed the stairs. She had no booty to speak of and no titties, either. I wasn't attracted to women who had bodies like twelve-year-old boys. I liked flesh, and this woman was mostly having a hard time filling out her Calvins. (Her jeans weren't Calvins; they wouldn't be good enough for her.)

We got upstairs and I wondered if she, like Allison, had moved back in. Well, there was more than enough room in that joint to make Allison, Edina and all their friends nice and comfy.

She stood at a closed bedroom door and threw it open, then she motioned for me to enter. I felt pretty sure she didn't want to ride my dick, but she seemed at that moment like one of those strung-out, decadent hookers I had busted so many times.

IT'S ALL GOOD

9

"Sit," she said.

"Yes, Mistress Edina." I sat. "Please don't hurt me. I been hurt a lot."

She lit up a Newport and smoked, pacing back and forth. Then she stubbed it out and lit up another one.

"Well, it's been fun watching you smoke," I said, rising, "but I have places to go and things to do."

"Coolidge, don't go," she said. "I'm sorry, I was just being a bitch."

I sat back down. "OK, I'm here, you're here. Let's talk."

"Want a drink?"

"No, I don't want a fuckin' drink. Your mother just poured so much tea down my throat that I'm gonna need to take a long piss real soon. So, let's talk about your family business and its recent fire."

"What's happened between you and Lloyd? I mean, there's this fire, and you're the investigator and he's the boss of the company. So why don't you ask him?"

"Well, he seems very unwilling to talk to me, and I'm here and you're here, so why don't you talk to me about it? After all, your mother promised me you would cooperate with me. Plus, your brother thinks maybe you're part of the bad stuff that goin' on."

"My brother," she said, "is a prick."

"Look," I said, taking a deep breath and trying hard not to get an attitude, "when I was a cop, I hated dealing with people who wouldn't answer my questions. As a private eye, I get fed up with people who pull that same kind of bullshit with me. Right now, I think you're being difficult just for the hell of it. So I'm gonna ask some questions, and you're gonna answer them. Hear me?"

Her face went whiter and harder. "I hoped you wouldn't be like that."

"Like *what*? I don't what's goin' on, and whatever it is, it concerns *me* personally, and the more I find out about it the more it freaks me out. I'm a desperate man who needs some answers."

"You seem to think our family is somehow responsible for the fire. Why is that?"

"Well, who else might be behind it? I'm wide open to suggestions."

"We have plenty of competitors." She took a deep drag of her cigarette and held it in, as if she were smoking weed. I could tell how much the nicotine soothed her. She would probably smoke for the rest of her life. Her face was narrow and her features fine. I could see no lines in her face. Maybe she had spent some of that Norman money on facelifts, or maybe she had just decided never to do human things like smile, laugh or frown, because that would put lines in her face. It was weird for me to know that she and Allison had come from the same family. Allison was good-natured, optimistic, endlessly tolerant and eager to become everyone's best friend. Edina, meanwhile, was lean and mean, nothing but edges and angles and attitude. So she stood there in that bedroom, smoking and looking at me, and I thought, *Is she checking me out?* Maybe she was saying to herself, *Hey, Coolidge, is it true what they say about your kind? I mean, all those times when you were hanging out with Allison, were you just friends? Or were you slipping her the hot beef injection? I'll bet you have a big black bone swinging between those legs. How about letting me take a peek? Better still, why don't you take me for a ride?*

She said, "I don't suppose you'll fill me in on what my mother said to you."

"Don't you people speak to each other in your family?"

"Not often, and not about anything as serious as this."

"Well, when I find out what's happening, I'll be more than happy to call you and tell you everything I know. But as a former police officer and current private investigator, I have learned that it's a pretty good idea not to run all over town telling everyone everything I know."

Edina's big eyes twinkled with mirth. I have a gift for overstatement and understatement that wins people over.

"You OK with that?" I asked her.

"Yes, fine."

"You look like you're ready to laugh at me."

"Not at all. It's just that you're so much like I remember you when you and Allison were friends. You'd come over and you were so young and feisty and you just said what was on your mind. We didn't know anyone else who was remotely like you. In our circle, we kept ours mouth shut."

I just shrugged. If she wanted some kind of retort from me, well, she wasn't gonna get it.

"I know why you're here." She looked down at the carpet, sounding humble. "I respect that you're in a difficult position and you've come to us to get answers in order to extricate yourself from your predicament. I'm sure my mother enjoyed visiting with you—she thought you were a charming young man years ago and I'm sure she feels the same way now—and I appreciate your good manners. If, while you're investigating, you would give me updates, that would be terrific. Fair enough?"

I nodded. "You said something about how all this trouble may be caused by someone outside the company. What did you mean?"

She waited a moment, then spoke. "I know of one person who hates us all. There was a guy who worked for us years ago, a mechanical engineer named Huey Capwell. Just before my father died, Huey killed himself."

"Did anyone believe that your family was somehow responsible for the suicide?"

"Yes, Huey's wife. Apparently she thought that Lloyd had much to do with it. You'd have to ask one of the others about it. I was in Europe then, and when I heard about it, I thought, 'Oh, that's awful.

Let's talk about something else.'" She shuddered at the memory as she stubbed out her cigarette.

"So Lloyd was such a bully that Huey couldn't cope with him and committed suicide?"

"Actually, the widow said right off that Lloyd murdered Huey."

"For real?"

"Well, Lloyd would have had a motive. Huey had been with the company a long time and knew the ins and outs of air conditioning as well as anyone. He also had a headful of ideas about how to improve current appliances and build innovative new ones. He was going to jump ship and start his own company based on what he had learned from working for us. His desertion would have hurt our business a great deal."

I shook my head. "Even someone like Lloyd Norman doesn't kill a man for saying, 'I'm gonna take what I've learned from you and start a business to compete against you.' Shit, man, that happens every day in this country."

"You didn't know Huey Capwell and what an asset he was to our company and what a dangerous competitor he could have been."

I sighed. "Edina, that's some serious trash you're talking about your own brother. I've been a cop, and now I'm a private eye. I know people, and what you've just told me is…no, Lloyd wouldn't do it."

"Coolidge, I'm just telling you what I heard. I was told that Huey's widow believed that Lloyd had killed him."

"Didn't the police make some sort of investigation?"

"I guess they did. But I was in Europe and didn't

want to know about any of it. You should contact them about it."

"Oh, I will. You never know what you'll find out when you go to the authorities and start asking questions. Where is Missus Capwell now?"

"Some said she left town, but I don't know. I know she was from out of state and maybe, after Huey died, she split. I do know that she was a bartender by training."

"Anybody else who wanted to off him?"

"Nope."

"What about you? You came back to the States because Lloyd was mismanaging the company, right?"

She smiled, as if I'd started playing games with her by asking such a direct, serious question. "I came back because I heard bad things about Lloyd and our company .I wanted to check them out while there was something left of the company."

"And what were you gonna do if things were as bad as you heard?"

"Get Lloyd's incompetent ass out of there."

"So, if he ends up being charged with fraud, it won't surprise you."

"Not at all. It would just tell me that he couldn't even get away with having someone torch his warehouse. I want to take over as president of Norman Appliances. I would do a much better job than Lloyd. But I wouldn't do anything unethical or illegal to get the presidency."

I half-expected her to punctuate her little speech with a wink.

"I respect your honesty," I half-lied. Her flippancy annoyed me. I had expected, and wanted, her to get pissed and go on a tirade during which she would go temporarily insane and start telling me things she new she should keep to herself. Instead, she made a joke of our conversation, practically laughing at me. Allison once told me that Edina, in high school, had been "a slut," a poor little rich girl who said and did every kind of outrageous thing. "She smoked weed, talked back to adults and had a different boyfriend every fifteen minutes," said Allison. "She knew she could get away with acting out because she was a Norman. She would always have all the goodies she wanted and she didn't have to conform."

So that was the woman who stood before me, and I had very little patience with such people. I made a point of looking at my watch and said, "It's after six. I better be going."

Back in my car, I felt very hungry again. That tea and those fag sandwiches had been a nice snack, but no meal, especially for a man my size. So I pulled into the nearest McDonald's drive through and bought a Big Mac, fries and a Coke. Normally I didn't eat junk food, but normally I didn't let myself get famished, either. I sat in the parking lot and devoured the empty calories in two or three minutes. It went down fast and nice, and I promised myself I wouldn't eat that shit again until the next time.

Back at my microloft, I felt that mild but unrelenting loneliness that started when Emma flew off to Philly. Usually I don't allow myself to indulge in self-pity because I think that self-pity is something for weak, sniveling little people. I enjoy being single and living by myself. I think the greatest guy in the world to hang out with is Cool Jones. I think aloneness is a healthful thing and I can find a hundred ways to entertain myself. Except that none of them seemed like much fun. I knew I didn't need to see a shrink or take meds—when I was a cop, I knew many others who needed that kind of help but were always in denial about it. Still, I went to bed not long after dinnertime, and I thought that was a pretty fuckin' lame thing to do. I was a badass private eye on a crusade to stamp out all evil and make the world a beautiful place for women and children.

10

By one o'clock the following day, I had located Brandy Capwell in the Midwesterner, a bar in O'Hare International Airport. I had her number, literally, and kept her busy slamming down the phone in my ear as she poured drinks. Last year I'd had to pop someone a couple of times and the unbearably loud noise from that experience had fucked up my ears. Before hanging up on me the second or third time, she had told me where to go and what to do with myself once I got there. I found her remark somewhat offensive.

I had started that morning with a call to the union representing bartenders and food service workers, and they told me jackshit. I'm old enough to remember the world before 9/11, when a person could call a number and get whatever information he needed. Then they passed the Patriot Act into law, which gives Uncle Sam the right to stick his nose into everyone's business—like he didn't already have such rights before—and everyone has gotten so paranoid. You might say, "Good morning! How are you?" and they'll say, "What's it to ya?" So, for a private investigator who's trying to get some facts that will allow him to put together the pieces of a jigsaw puzzle, his job has become much more difficult if he doesn't use all the means at his disposal.

A good way around all that aggravation is the Internet. I pay LexisNexis and Intelius, and they tell me what's goin' on. If I want to know how often Jane Doe drops a deuce, they'll give it up to me. So I sat there in my microloft in San Francisco, wanting to speak to someone named Brandy Capwell, but I had no clear idea of where she was. But I did have her name, and hers was a relatively uncommon name, so that meant I had a lot. I logged into the online services and they were quite happy to tell me that Brandy, related to Huey, had lived in Oakland but now was in Chicago, and here was her work phone number. Did I want her Social Security Number and birthdate, too? No problem.

Shit, I thought. This was almost as good as sex. It was definitely better than safe sex.

A woman answered. "Hello?"

"May I speak to Brandy Capwell?"

"Speaking."

"Great," I said with a little laugh.

"Who's calling?" She sounded a little nasty. Maybe I would, too, if I was Brandy Capwell and had some deep-voiced black dude on the phone asking for me.

I was very surprised to reach her personally, so I hadn't prepared myself with which lies to tell. I made the stupid mistake of being honest. "My name is Coolidge Jones, and I'm a private investigator in San Francisco—"

Boom! went the phone. *Ouch!* went my ear. I dialed her again, but this time she wouldn't answer it. I knew I should go to SFO and fly out to Chicago for a personal meeting with Brandy. If I'd been working for a client, I would have done so without hesitation, for the simple reason that I am totally OK with spending other people's money. But my own money is another matter, because I am very stingy.

I went down to the police station. Roberta Johnson, who usually tells me the shit I'm not supposed to know, was still out of town. The man sitting in for her, Danny Alvarez, took forever to do things and was reluctant to give me information that I apparently couldn't get on my own. So I walked right past him and headed for Marsha in Records, who also isn't supposed to give me any little favors. Marsha, a tall, spare black woman, shakes her head whenever she sees me because she knows what I'm up to, and what I'm up to is the same things that all other private investigators are up to: gaining some access to confidential police records.

"What you want now, Coolidge?"

"What up, Marsha?" I asked, leaning over the counter.

She sat at her computer and spoke to me without looking up. "It's all good, Coolidge. You come by just to say hidy?"

"I need a favor."

"You know I'm married."

"Not *that* kind of favor."

"Then I don't wanna hear it."

We both laughed. That fuckin' Marsha could always bust my onions. "I want to know about a suicide from a couple of years back," I said.

"Bridge jumper?" she asked.

"No. His name was Huey Capwell."

Marsha looked up at me.

"You've heard of Huey Capwell?" I asked her.

Marsha gave the special little look she reserved for dummies: She nodded with much exaggeration, her chin dropping almost to her chest, her mouth wide open. If you didn't know her, you would swear she was a drooling retard.

"Talk to me, Marsha."

"Lieutenant Lando still gets mad about that one. Huey Capwell is this suicide, right? So what happens? They lose all the evidence, including the body. Some people at the hospital got fired because of it. Then the man's widow has the body cremated lickety-split, so by the time we figure out that the body's disappeared, it's burned and floating in the ocean."

I shook my head and blew out a breath. "I can't believe I didn't already know that."

"Well, now you do. Lieutenant Lando got so mad about the whole thing. He's yelling, 'Somebody screwed up and lost Huey Capwell's body!' But nobody can figure out who did it. The doctor went all through Memorial Hospital looking for the body." Marsha paused. "The decedent's widow sure seemed in a hurry to have the cremation done. Wonder what was up with *that*."

"I'm surprised Lando got so mad about it. It was a suicide, right? No question about it?"

"Far as Lieutenant Lando is concerned, there is *always* a question. Now, you better git before Lando comes by or *I'll* be in trouble."

I headed out to Memorial Hospital and had a visit with a pathology technician I had known for a while. He told me much of what Marsha had said.

"Here is our protocol," he added. "A courier comes by in a van to collect to collect specimens from labs and law-enforcement agencies. Those specimens were sealed and labeled, then put in cold packs. The stuff then sat in the lab's refrigerator until the driver arrived for it. He signed for it before he drove off.

"The Huey Capwell remains?" He shook his head. "I don't know what happened there. Everyone who deals with these specimens and cadavers knows what to do and not to. The clerk here at Memorial says she did it the regular way and can't imagine why things went wrong. The courier also swore that he got what he was supposed to get, signed for it all and delivered it. Nobody knew anything was the matter until Doctor Yenson called days later and said, 'I want a progress report on the remains of Huey Capwell.' Well, they looked around and couldn't find the body or anything else. He had been cremated by then."

In Memorial's lobby, I took out my iPhone and called my travel agent, Juan. I told him I needed a return ticket to O'Hare as soon as possible.

"If you're in a hurry to get to Chicago, and I can't imagine why," he said, "the most efficient way is for you to go to SFO, then take a shuttle down to San Jose and get their Chicago flight because it's direct."

I did some very fast thinking. If I took Jose's advice, I would get to O'Hare at about ten-thirty at night, and Brandy, if she started working at three, would get off at eleven. I flashed on myself, curling up and trying to sleep on a plastic seat at O'Hare because I didn't want to spend a couple of hundred dollars for a hotel room over and above the plane ticket I'd just paid for. In my wallet I had twelve dollars and my American Express card. I was pretty much living off my plastic. I had about thirty-five cents in my checking account. Shitfuck!

"Let's do it, Juan."

"Done."

I drove down to San Francisco International Airport and boarded the aircraft with damn close to fifteen minutes to spare. The aircraft was puny and held not more than a dozen passengers. They started up the engines and I thought how wimpy they sounded. Could we really stay airborne all the way to San Jose? I didn't like to fly. My ears popped like motherfuckers and it freaked me out that those jumbo jets could stay at 30,000 feet for hours at a time.

But we did get there, as promised. It took us only about twenty minutes, and my Delta flight to the Windy City took off minutes after I boarded it. The aircraft held many crying babies and people with really goofy Midwestern accents. The lunch was cold and unidentifiable. The cocktails made me snooze for an hour or so, and I woke up just before we landed. I waited till everyone left the aircraft, then I half-ran off the plane, went to the first information person I could find, got the disappointing news that the Midwesterner, where Brandy worked, was at the other end of O'Hare. I walked as fast as I could, which was pretty damn fast. I reached my destination at five minutes after Brandy Capwell had left. She would be back in two days.

"Shitfuck!" I said aloud, not giving a good goddamn who overheard.

11

So I did the only thing I could do: I got to the information booth to page Brandy. I passed by their booth, approached a uniformed woman who could have passed for Rosie O'Donnell's older sister. I wasn't sure what kind of "assistance" she was supposed to provide, and I guessed *she* didn't rightly know, either, so that was good for me. The woman was clearly locking up for the night and rolled her eyes a little bit when I told her I needed to page someone.

"Ma'am," I said, "I've just flown in from San Francisco to see someone who is on her way out of O'Hare at this moment. I don't know which exit she'll be using. I *really* need to have her paged. Can you help me?"

The white woman looked me up and down, as so many others had and countless others will till I die, and she frowned at this big black man who seemed so desperate to find some "Brandy Capwell" before Brandy made it to the parking lot. Concluding that I was neither a rapist nor a stalker, the info lady got on the phone, gave them the information I had given her, and soon I heard "Brandy Capwell, please come to the information booth" broadcast throughout one of the world's biggest airports.

"Thank you, thank you," I said, Uncle Tomming it up a little for her. She just gathered up her coat and purse, nodded a little in my direction and took off for home.

I did not know if Brandy Capwell would respond to the page. Maybe, like Elvis, she had already left the building. Or maybe she had heard the announcement but thought, *Fuck it. I'm too tired to go all that way to the information desk. If it's that important, they will find me sooner or later.*

Just for the hell of it, I entered the information booth and sat down on the soft leather chair. I checked the time: a little over ten minutes had passed. Time sure passes fast when you want it to stay put. I rooted through a couple of drawers that were unlocked and found a brochure advertising "Chicago's finest dinner," with a picture of a prime rib of beef, veggies, a glass of wine and a slice of cheesecake. I wiped drool from my chin and heard my stomach growl like a junkyard dog.

"Is this the right booth? I heard the page, so here I am." The accent was nasal, Midwestern. Brandy Capwell stood before me, trim, compact, swarthy.

Long dark hair, strong features, more handsome than pretty. I got up and smiled. She had on a burgundy blouse and black slacks, a typical bartender's uniform. She must have removed her name tag.

"Hello? What's the deal, honey? Is there another booth I don't know about?" She smirked. "Are you the new guy here? You're not exactly dressed for it."

"I'm not the new guy here," I told her. "I'm an old guy from out there." I extended my hand. "Pleased to meet you, Missus Capwell."

She looked at me sideways and slowly gave me her hand, as if she were afraid that I would crush her hand with my own and jerk her arm away, dislocating her shoulder. Now, would I do a thing like that? Well, yes. I had done it half a dozen times before, to folks who had it coming.

Well, I gave her hand a nice little shake.

"I still don't know who you are," she said.

"I'm from San Francisco. I called you at work. You hung up the phone."

She snatched her hand out of mine. "I thought you knew that I didn't want to talk to you. I sure hope you didn't fly all the way out here just to have this little confrontation with me."

"Yes, ma'am. That's just what I did. You'd just left your workplace when I got there. So I had you paged here so that we could talk. You think maybe we could get a cup of coffee and talk a little while?"

"We're talking right now."

"I don't think we're supposed to be at this booth. I thought we could sit and talk for a spell."

"Talk about what?"

"I'm wondering about your husband's death."

Her eyes narrowed. "You with the media? You

want to write a book about Huey's death?"

"Actually, I'm a private investigator."

"Oh, I see. Who put you up to this?"

"I put myself up to it. I was working for an insurance company, and there was a fire at Norman Appliances' warehouse. Huey Capwell's name was getting tossed around. I'm really hoping you can tell me something about how he died."

We stayed silent for a moment. Brandy stared at my shirt, then at the floor. Now she knew what I was after, and she probably wanted to cooperate with me, yet also probably had good reason not to do so.

"What's that fire got to do with Huey?"

I shrugged. "Maybe nothing, maybe something. Everyone back there thought it was weird that his remains disappeared. No samples of his tissues. Everyone wondered what happened."

"Shit happened, that's all," she said. "Look, since you've come all this way, I'll go have a drink with you. Half an hour. I'll answer your questions. Deal?"

"OK."

We ended up at the nearest airport bar and sat by the huge window, protected from the rain that had started. It could rain in torrents but the aircraft would still arrive and depart; hell, a blizzard could start and I doubt they would close down O'Hare.

Brandy excused herself to make a cell phone call. I ordered each of us a glass of white wine. She sure took her own sweet fuckin' time with that call.

Then I heard footsteps and she was back. "Sorry about that. My roomie is having a personal crisis and needed a little bit more of my time than usual." She plopped down into her seat and sighed. Just then I noticed she had removed her burgundy blouse and now wore only a white T-shirt. She took a big sip of wine and, without any self-consciousness, tugged at her T-shirt to air herself out, as if she were with a bunch of girlfriends.

"Roommate's a head case, huh? Why not get your own crib?"

"With these rents? I can barely make do as it is. I need someone to pay half the rent."

I smiled. She had mellowed out and decided to chill with me for a little bit. I had seen that before, especially as a cop. The civilian in distress is telling you to fuck off; when you don't fuck off, and instead you are perfectly willing to hear what they have to say, they take you into their confidence and make you their newest best friend. One of my guilty pleasures as a police officer was being around people who had been victimized; who could resist watching a good freakout?

"We better talk fast and drink fast if we have to do this in half an hour," I said.

Brandy shook her head. "Never mind that. Maggie's overdosed again on Tylenols. She gets all dopey and falls asleep, then wakes up fifteen hours later. She's done this two dozen times. I come home, she's in a stupor, I call the paramedics and they do their thing. She's a decent-looking woman, and tragic, too. She's dated a few of the paramedics. I guess it's just her thing, her way of getting attention."

"So," I said, "tell me about Huey."

"We met when he was forty and I was twenty-one. I took the bus out to San Francisco when I was twenty-one. Most girls take the bus out to Los Angeles at that age because they want to become movie or TV stars. But not me. I went to bartending school and then started working at a bar at SFO. I don't know why I've made a career out of working at airport bars, but that's how it's worked out. Over time I met Huey while I was at work. He came in for a drink, we got to talking and we fell in love and got married. We lasted a long time and were happy till the end. I knew that man as well as I knew myself. He did not kill himself. He was too high on life."

"How can you be so sure?"

"How can *you* be so sure that when you go back home the Golden Gate Bridge will still be there? You just *know* about some things."

"So you think he was murdered."

"Yes, sir, that's what I'm thinkin'. Lloyd Norman did it to him, but of course he won't admit it and his family has got his back twenty-four/seven. Have you talked to them?"

"A little bit. I heard about Huey's death just yesterday."

"I'm pretty sure that the Normans paid off everyone necessary to make sure that Lloyd would get away with it. They have unlimited money and know everyone in Frisco that's worth knowing."

"Brandy," I said, "these are the Normans you're talking about. A very respected family that would never do the things you're accusing them of doing."

She hooted. "Coolidge, were you born yesterday? One of the Normans kills someone, so of *course* his family is going to do everything to protect him. I'm sure that you believe that. Otherwise, you wouldn't have gone to all this trouble and expense to talk to me."

"I don't know nothin'," I told her. "That's why I'm sittin' in O'Hare with someone I've never met, tryin' to figure out the death of someone I'd never met."

"Well, I'll help you out: They killed him. It was not suicide, he was not mentally ill. He loved his life and he loved his wife, and looked forward to living a few more decades at least."

"OK, here's some more that I heard: He wanted to jump ship and start his own company based on what he had learned while working at Norman."

"Oh, he *talked* about plenty of things—how he was gonna do this and that. He had worked for Guy Norman for so many years, and Huey was a very loyal employee. But it was clear to everyone that Guy was going to appoint Lloyd as the company's next boss. Huey said, 'Lloyd couldn't run a bath, much less a company.'"

"Did Guy and Huey have any confrontations over that matter?"

"I know that Huey tried to quit, but Guy said, 'We've been together too long. I won't accept your resignation.' Plus, around that time, the Army decided to buy zillions of new air conditioners, and Guy said, 'Huey, if we get that contract, I'll need you to supervise that order.' So Huey said he'd just bide his time and see if Norman got that contract. Then, a couple of days after that, I came home and found him in his car, dead. I could tell that he hadn't just nodded off in his car."

"So there is absolutely, positively no way his death could have been an accident?"

She leaned forward. "Hello? Have you been listening? I said he wanted to live, love and learn. He thought the world revolved around Huey Capwell. He couldn't have imagined depriving us of the pleasure of his company."

"How can you be sure," I asked her, "that he didn't have some shit goin' on in his life that he kept secret from you?"

She shrugged but said nothing.

"I can't buy this murder thing," I said. "There's no reason for Lloyd to kill him. No reason at all. Lloyd wasn't even the boss yet."

Brandy shrugged again. "I figured the murder was because Lloyd was paranoid enough to say, 'If Huey quits and starts his own business, he'll destroy Norman Appliances. Better just kill him and the problem is solved.'"

"People don't do things like that. Huey hadn't quit, and probably would have stayed at Norman Appliances for the rest of his career. That's what I think."

"And I'm tellin' you what *I* think."

I sighed. "I hear ya, and I'm not callin' you a liar. But I don't think it was a murder. If it was, Lloyd wasn't necessarily the guy who did it."

"I think it was Lloyd. I don't know for sure. I wish I did. I'll never know. But the thing that matters is, life goes on. Huey is dead. All these questions you're asking me? I'm thinking, 'It doesn't matter anymore.'"

"Brandy, why did you have him cremated so soon?"

She shook her head. "It wasn't me. Huey wanted to be cremated. He had been dead for a couple of days. The coroner released him and the guy at the funeral home said, 'Let's do the cremation.' So I said, 'OK, let's do it.' When you get back to Frisco, ask the funeral guy about it. Maybe he remembers.

"They drugged him to trigger a heart attack or

something," Brandy continued. "Then they got rid of all of his remains, even the tissue and blood samples."

"Maybe he was drunk and died of acute alcohol poisoning."

"He had stopped drinking years earlier."

"Did he have a drinking problem?"

"He was in recovery. Remember, we *met* in an airport bar on a Wednesday at two-thirty in the afternoon. He'd come all the way out to SFO just for that. I said, 'When is your flight? Where are you headed?' He said, 'I don't have a flight to catch. I'm not going anywhere. I just want to sit here and drink and watch the planes.' Pretty sad, huh? Well, I fell in love with him, and when you're in love, you just don't see the person's flaws. It took me years so see how fucked up he was. He got into some recovery program and stayed sober for the rest of his life."

"Maybe he had a relapse."

"Not him. The doctor had him on Antabuse. It would have made him violently ill if he'd started drinking again."

"You sure he took the stuff?"

"Sure I'm sure. He took it in front of me each morning."

"How many people knew about his Antabuse?"

"I dunno. He didn't go around telling people, 'I'm a drunk who's on meds.' If people were drinking, he'd have an iced tea."

"Do you remember if everything was OK during the week he died?"

"It was just another week. He went to work, spoke to Guy…and then he died. After the funeral, I packed up and headed back here and haven't gone anywhere since. My life is divided between my apartment and the O'Hare bar I work at. It's very boring."

"After Huey died, and you went through his things, did you find a note or anything?"

"No. Murdered men don't leave suicide notes."

12

My flight back to SFO was mostly boring. Brandy and I had talked for close to two hours, she went home and I wandered through the vastness of O'Hare Airport until my legs got sore, then I sat and let myself think happy thoughts till my brain got sore and announced it wanted to go to bed. I smiled for a few minutes at the memories of my all-nighters as a young stud with my boys and our bitches, the booze and weed and dancing…then my brain reminded me that I was a middle-aged private eye who no longer had the stamina and resiliency to party all night, then work all day. So I sat there till I dozed off, and when I woke up I felt no better at all. I had recorded my talk with Brandy on my iPhone, and now believed that

Huey had been murdered, though I was goddamned if I knew the details. But if he had been murdered, it probably had something to do with his activities at Norman Appliances.

As I ate my bland breakfast and the jumbo jet rocked from turbulence, I concluded that my trip to Chi-town had been a good idea. I thanked Brandy for not being a cunt; she'd taken my email address and given me hers, so that if one of us learned something worth knowing, they could contact the other. I had asked lots of questions that she couldn't answer, but I was OK with that. As long as I had questions that *someone* could answer, I could stay busy. I got pissed off when the person said, "I don't know, and I don't know who *does* know." With Huey Capwell, I'd gotten some answers and knew what my next questions should be. That's when work became fun.

My flight arrived at SFO at around six in the morning. I had napped during the flight and felt moderately rested as I got into my car and drove back into the city. Still, after I'd parked and entered my microloft, I flopped into bed fully dressed and conked out within five minutes.

At just after nine, I woke up because someone had started pounding on my door. My mouth tasted as if a sewer rat had dropped a deuce into it and I cringed at the smell of my own stale sweat. I went the whole two steps it took to reach my door and used the peephole. I wasn't in the mood to beat the shit out of any bad guy this early in the morning. Standing at my door was no bad guy; it was worse. It was my second ex, Aja Harvey.

"What the *fuck*?" I muttered. I looked again at the distorted image the tiny hole provided. All I could see was her coffee-colored face and frizzy dark sort-of-African hair cut short. Aja Harvey is probably—no, definitely, and unfortunately—the foxiest woman I have ever met, and I have met some of the foxiest women in California, a place that is known for the foxiness of its women. Beautiful women, many times, are bad news. They don't give a shit about anyone but themselves and they never let you get in to use the bathroom. I like a women with a sweet face, a kind face, a different face, but not Aja's kind of *Vogue*-meets-Hollywood flawless thing: big brown eyes, small, straight nose, perfect white teeth—and don't get me started on her dimpled smile.

I opened the door. "Aja?"

"What up, Cool?"

I gave her my best fuck-off stare, hoping she would lose her nerve and walk away. She was tall and slim, with everything just where it should be. She ate like Oprah but never gained weight nor got bad skin. The cheeseburgers, ice cream and beer went in one hole and out the other. That day, she had on ripped, faded jeans and a white T-shirt that showed off her burnished-ebony complexion. Just another one of California's black beauties, and a singer who should have been famous by now. The first time I saw her, she was rocking the house at a North Beach bar. I don't remember which part of her I fell in love with at first. Probably all at the same time.

"How'd you get in?" I asked her as we stood there.

"Front door was ajar." Beautiful voice, low and smoky.

"Why'd you come back?"

She gave a little shrug. "It's kinder and gentler here. Brutal out there. You look beat to shit, Cool."

"Fuck you very much."

She laughed, the sort of sexy laugh that was uniquely Aja's. She looked me up and down, as if searching for traces of the lovesick child I once had been. "You've shaved your head."

"Been shavin' it for a while. Makes me look tougher."

"Uh, I think I caught you at a time when you're not in the right frame of mind to deal with me," she said.

"Aja, why are you here? I haven't had as much sleep as I'm used to and I feel like a fuckin' zombie."

"I have great news," she said.

"Yeah?"

"Mama's clean!" she smiled and arched her eyebrows. "No crack, no smack, no meth, no Jack Daniels for a year now. It's been hard, but I'm toughing it out."

"Nice for you," I said.

"Jesus, can't you be more supportive of me?"

"Couldn't *you* have been more supportive of *me* when we were married?"

She gave a little sigh and squinted at me. "Coolidge, do the words 'second chance' mean anything to you?"

"Aja, do the words 'lying bitch' mean anything to *you*?"

She rolled her eyes a little bit, the way she always had when being spoken to with major disrespect. "I've been through therapy. I know how to deal with shit. Maybe you should check it out, too. Want her number?"

"What I *want*," I said, "is for you to go away."

"You mean I can't come in?"

"No you fucking can't!"

"Coolidge, what's up with that anger? We've been apart for five years—"

"Eight."

"OK, so it's been eight ears. So I'm, like, 'What's with all that anger, guy? I mean, I'm not mad at *you* for anything."

"Aja, there's this word, 'sociopath.' Look it up. It means you."

She pouted and looked at the ground. She wasn't getting whatever she wanted from me. What *did* she want? As much as she could get, and more. Like so many other sociopaths, she could jerk people around, go away for a long time, then return and say, 'Hi! It's me! I've come to exploit you some more!' Then they really *don't* understand why you're not thrilled to see them again.

"I wasn't expecting this attitude, Coolidge. I mean, we had fun. We did some shit. Right?"

"Better get your hands away while I slam this door."

Boom. I went back to bed and tried to sleep, but now I was too worked up about her visit and all the things I needed to do that day. I got up and shit, showered and shaved. I put on some fresh clothes and sat on my bed for a few minutes, admitting to myself how many times I had daydreamed about her coming back to me, and what clever things I would say to her. So, it had just happened, and I handled it in a way I thought was totally unsatisfactory, and now she was gone, and I wished she would come back, because during our little visit I could feel some of the things I had felt when I was in love with her. When she left me eight years earlier, she took some precious parts of me with her, parts I could not grow back, and I took out my rage and hurt on those around me. Roberta, the closest thing I had to a girlfriend, blew off my moodiness as if it were dust on an old coast. She had *her* attitude, too, so our shit went together OK most of the time. For the longest while, I thought I had my past kept securely out of sight and usually not thought of, but then it knocked on my door and flashed its big dimpled smile.

I got on the phone to Ophelia Terryman and made arrangements to check her out later that day. Then I did some office things and wished I still had an office. By noon, I felt ready to do some errands. I went downstairs to get my car and saw Aja, on Turk Street, waiting in her piece-of-shit ride, gazing in my direction. I pulled out and drove off, feeling particularly pissed that in addition to having lost my rent-free office, I now felt my ex was stalking me.

At about dinnertime, I found the Terrymans' home in spite of myself. Their crib, hidden by two tons of leaves and concrete, was on one of those tucked-away lanes in Lafayette. They had a locked gate and a hedge tall enough to make sure the have-nots couldn't get a peek at their front lawn. I buzzed and they let me in, lucky me.

I knocked on the door, expecting a black woman in a uniform to answer and say, "What you want, fool? We ain't expectin' no deliveries today." Instead, Ophelia opened the door.

"Hello, Coolidge. Cody is on his way. We have a cocktail party to go to. Come on in."

"If this is a bad time—"

"Not at all. Let's talk."

We walked to the back of the house. Ophelia, like

the rest of the Normans except Allison, was tall and skinny, with good features. Not much in the way of titties or booty. Her blonde hair ended just above her shoulders. She struck me as being much friendlier than Edina, which was no big deal, but she was no salt-of-the-earth Allison. I didn't think there were many people in the world as down and warm as Allison.

"Coolidge, it's been a decade at least. What have you been doing?"

"I'm a private investigator," I said.

"Married with kids?"

"I tried marriage a couple of times. Didn't work out. No kids. You got any?"

She laughed. "Kids? No, thanks."

I looked around and thought Ophelia's house was like dozens of others. That *Architectural Digest* feature on Danielle Steel's Washington Street mansion made me feel that everyone else's house was ordinary.

"So," she said as we sat, "what's on your mind?"

"Norman Appliances is on my mind. What do you know about it?"

She frowned. "Not too much. Cody does the worrying for both of us. Lloyd has been running things but Edina thinks he's doing a poor job. She wants my support in her plan to take over for him. Lloyd will shit if that happens, but too bad for him."

"Are you going to help Edina if she tries to unseat Lloyd?"

"I guess. She could run the company much better than he does. She's smarter and works harder. You've probably been told that Lloyd thinks the company is so stable and respected that it runs itself and is totally indestructible. Well, he *does* think that, but he's wrong.

Cody's always talking about how big, strong American companies fail because overseas competition comes in and steals too many customers. So Cody is saying, 'Lloyd wants to expand into home air conditioning and RV air conditioning, but those market niches are already taken. We would lose a fortune.' Lloyd's judgment is very poor and he won't listen to why his ideas would fail. Edina wants, at least, to make sure that Lloyd can't do anything as president of the company without consulting the rest of us."

"What about Brynne?"

"Just wants to party and doesn't give a shit what's going on so long as there's a party going on."

"What about Allison? Whose side is she on?"

"Allison just wants to do the right thing."

"Your mother probably doesn't like this very much."

"My mother is quite disgusted by all of it. She thinks it would be best just to leave things be and let Lloyd pretend he's the boss of Norman Appliances. He really is harmless when he just stands around looking like a big shot."

"Is Lloyd honest and ethical?"

She snorted. "Absolutely not. That's why we want to put limits on his power. He's such a bullshit artist."

"So y'all don't get along?"

"He's family, so I guess I love him, but I dislike him very much. He's bossy and suspicious and convinced he's right and everyone else is wrong. He doesn't understand much about the business he's in but he's too stubborn to admit it. He wears ugly suits and his cologne smells awful."

"Have you heard anything about that warehouse blaze? That's the reason I'm here," I said.

"Just what Cody's said. He told me that Lloyd borrowed money a couple of years ago. He used the company as collateral. Well, we've had this global economic downturn and everyone's been hurting. Lloyd personally has been losing money. That half-million from the warehouse fire? It would be very nice."

"Do you think he did it?"

"I honestly don't know, and I couldn't care less. I'm not interested in Norman Appliances. I'm interested in going places, doing things, laughing and having a good time."

I smiled. "Sounds like fun."

She smiled back. "It has its moments. There are people who would say, 'Ophelia Terryman is a spoiled brat,' and they'd be right. But I'm happy. I have the things I want and I *value* the things I have. Most people don't know *what* they want in the first place."

Just then, Cody Terryman appeared in the doorway.

"Hello, Coolidge. Ophelia said you would be coming by. I'm going to take a shower." To his wife, he said, "How about getting us a drink?"

He didn't say, "Come on! Chop, chop!" but she got to her feet and hustled off. I shook my head a little bit. If Aja Harvey had said that to me, I would have told her to get her own fuckin' drink.

IT'S ALL GOOD

13

I looked around the room and saw the things I had seen in other rich people's houses. I wondered if they had read the copy of *AD* that sat on the coffee table. I had read a dozen or so pages of a Danielle Steel novel because she owned and lived in the Spreckels mansion, a dozen or so blocks from my microloft and she had so much while I had so little. How had she sold hundreds of millions of copies of novels? After a dozen pages, I tossed her novel aside and promised myself I would never read another one.

Ophelia came back carrying a tray of goodies and a bottle of wine. Always hungry, I stared at the *hors d'oeuvres*, not knowing what was in those tasty treats, but not really caring, either. I wondered: If I gobbled them up myself, would these nice people be offended? I mean, they were gonna go to that cocktail party a little later on and chow down on tasty goodies all night, right? So why shouldn't I help myself right now?

Ophelia fussed around with the liquor bottles, turned down the lights and put on some Kenny G bullshit. She wore a fancy dress with a taffeta skirt that made a swooshing sound with every step she took. She had decent legs, small feet. Not much booty. Did she know Cool was checking out her booty? Did she like it? I bet she did.

I heard clack-clack-clack and there was Cody, all dressed up handsome, looking from Ophelia to me and back again, as if to remind me it was *his* house, *his* woman, I could enjoy *his* hospitality and ask my questions and then go home. His home and his woman were all very beautiful and very cold, and I wasn't allowed to touch anything.

Cody pointed to the tray of goodies. "After you, Coolidge."

I smiled. "Don't mind if I do."

I reached over, picked one up and stuffed it into my mouth. I still wasn't sure what it was, but it was way too yummy. I wiped tears from my eyes.

"Have another one," said Cody.

I nodded and did as he told.

"Ophelia, pour him some wine," said Cody.

She nodded and did as he told. The white wine was cold and delicious. I bet Danielle Steel ate and drank this primo shit every day.

Cody sat on the sofa and said, "I understand you have some questions about the warehouse fire."

"It seems that someone is trying to frame me, and

I need to know what you know about that fire."

Cody folded his arms and frowned. "Ask away."

"Tell me about Davida Avalon."

"For starters," Cody said with a grin, "I don't think she's an arsonist."

"I met her, and you, that day I went down to do the fire-scene inspection. She saw Clay give me that envelope full of paperwork I needed. That paperwork has since disappeared."

"I don't think Davida is a thief, either," he said.

"I'm not accusing anyone of anything," I told them. "Do Davida and Lloyd get along OK?"

"So far as I know. She's the office manager. She knows that part of her job is to get along with everyone."

"Davida thinks Lloyd is a goof-off," Ophelia said. "I mean, it's obvious that our father, who founded the company, forgot more about air conditioning than Lloyd has ever learned. But there are things that he *could* do but *doesn't* do because they bore him. Davida ends up doing them."

"Torching a warehouse is a serious thing," I said. "Lloyd must have had some pretty heavy enemies who wanted to do him like that. Think about it."

They both sat there, looking at the floor, then each other. They didn't know what to say, or maybe they did, but were damned if they were going to say it to *me*.

"What about that engineer who committed suicide?" I asked them.

"Huey Capwell," said Ophelia.

Cody frowned. "I got a call his widow from today."

"Brandy? For real? What did you talk about?" I

asked.

"*I* didn't talk—*she* did. Screamed, actually. Started carrying on about how I killed Huey. She was drunk or high, I think."

Ophelia shook her head. "I knew she thought Lloyd had killed him, but *you*? That woman really does need some Prozac or Adderall or something."

"Weird," I said. "Did she say anything concerning her whereabouts?"

"She said she was in Chicago," Cody told me, "and that Chicago wasn't far enough away from people like me. Then she starts saying something like, 'I've got half a mind to fly out there and punch you in the nose.'"

"Well," I said, "if she does show up here, tell her that, instead of punching you in the nose, she should call me. I have some questions for her." I, of course, withheld the fact that, hours earlier, I had drunk wine with Brandy at O'Hare and she made me believe that Lloyd had killed Huey.

"Speaking of flying in," Ophelia said to Cody, "did I tell you that Brynne is coming in tonight?"

"Wonderful," he said. "I hope you didn't buy her a plane ticket."

Ophelia laughed. "No, she has her own money, sort of. She owns part of the company. If she did need a handout, she'd probably get it from Edina." To me, she said, "Brynne is a cunt, pardon my French. She's very outspoken and her attitude is, 'I'll say what I want, whenever I want. If you don't like it, you can kiss my ass.' We had a big conflict last year and haven't spoken since."

She looked at Cody and he looked at her. Time's up, Cool.

I got up. "Well, I know you have places to go and things to do."

Cody got up, too. "I hope we haven't wasted your time."

I smiled. "It's all good. I'll leave you my card, and if you think of anything that might help, just call or email." I put my card on their coffee table.

Cody walked me to the door while Ophelia went to get her coat. "Coolidge," he said, "I didn't want to say this in front of my wife, but that phone call from Brandy Capwell? It freaked me out."

"Why?"

"She started *threatening* me over the phone."

"What did she say?"

"Something like, 'Have you ever wondered when you were going to die?' And I said, 'No, I think I have many years to go.' And she said, 'You never know when you're going to die. You just never know.'"

"And you really don't know why she contacted you?" I asked him.

"We haven't spoken since Huey died. She was a Chicagoan. She moved back home."

I nodded. "My understanding is that Brandy Capwell, at the time of Huey's death, had some concerns about how he died. She suspected murder. Maybe she still does."

"Yeah, she certainly does. But I hope *I'm* not the one she suspects."

"How well did you know Huey?"

Cody shrugged. "We worked together. We weren't chummy, but we got along. He worked hard, he took pride in being a good worker. That suicide thing struck me as unlikely. He had a sense of purpose in life. He was too busy living to give much thought to dying. Of course, he had problems at home, but he didn't bring his problems to work."

"What kind of problems at home?"

"Brandy had threatened to leave him. Didn't you know that?"

"All I know is what folks tell me."

"Huey was a nice guy," Cody said. "Maybe too nice. What's the word the shrinks use? 'Codependenr.' When Brandy wanted to cut him loose, well, I think it was hard for him. I don't know why she wanted to split. You should ask Lloyd about it. He might know."

Ophelia came back to us, wearing a bulky fur coat and carrying a man's dark-gray suit. "Cody," she said, "do you mind if I offer Coolidge this old suit of yours? It's been hanging there forever."

Cody nodded. "It was always kind of big for me. Take it, guy. It's a genuine Versace. *Haute couture.* Cost a fortune but I have plenty of others."

"Thanks, I'll take it," I said.

Cody said nothing more about Brandy Capwell as the three of us left the house together.

Outside, the clear, dark sky held a zillion stars and the weather was cold and windy. I liked northern California for just that reason—starry skies and blustery, cold nights turned me on. I took out my iPhone and called Mercedes at home. I wanted to drive to her place before going home, but she said not to bother; Vince had stayed late at work and she couldn't look through his office while he was there.

"I'll go in a little early tomorrow, before gets in, and see what I can find. I'll call you and tell you what's happening," she said.

After hanging up, I sat in the darkness of

Lafayette, listening to the wind blow against my old Ford. I squirmed as my 'roids started to itch and my eyelids felt leaden. Time for home and bed.

I got onto the westbound freeway and zipped across the Bay Bridge. Soon I was on Turk Street. So was Aja, unfortunately, still sitting in her car and wearing sunglasses. After I parked my car, she got out of hers and came up to me.

"Got a minute?"

"Not for you," I told her. I hated being an asshole and hated being around others who acted like assholes. I had been a police officer for years, and assholes went with the territory, but I never got to where I could honestly say, "I'm OK with that. Assholes are people, too."

"All right," I said. "Tell me what you want."

She smiled, Aja-style. All dimples and gleaming white teeth and twinkling brown eyes. "Chill, big man. I'm not gonna ask you for money and I'm not gonna offer to ride your dick."

"Then we have nothing to talk about." What I hated mostly were people who could turn me on and piss me off at the same time, and very few people had that power. Aja did.

"I need a little storage room," she said.

"For what?"

"I've taken up the harmonica, and I've gotten one of Bob Dylan's. It's vintage and is worth a lot, and its case is about the size of a laptop. If I leave it in that sorry-ass excuse for a car, someone will break in and rip me off."

"How did you manage to get a Dylan vintage harmonica? Didn't steal it, I hope."

She made a face. "No, I didn't fuckin' steal it. It's a

long story, and out here in the middle of Turk Street isn't the place to tell it." She paused. "I thought I might stay in town and try to get some singing gigs."

I glowered at her. "You drove up here all alone? No job, no money, no nothin'?"

She smirked. "Free country, right?"

"Why come to me?"

She just shrugged.

I sighed. We had had a hundred confrontations about her flakiness and my uptight-ness. She knew how much I adored her and wished to have her in my life even if she just kept taking bigger and bigger bites out of my ass.

I nodded. "OK, your harmonica can stay the night. Just make sure don't come by askin' for more favors." I must admit she hurt my feelings when she said she didn't want to ride my dick.

"That's fine, Cool. You're my boy."

"And just make sure there's no dope involved," I said.

"Mama's done ridin' the horse, baby."

"Mama *better* be." She knew I'd have her tossed in jail if she brought contraband into my home.

14

After popping a couple of Tylenol 3s, I flopped into bed and sank into a very deep sleep that rejuvenated my brain and body. I woke up at around six and got ready for a jog. Part of my preparation was to peek out the window to make sure Aja had gone away. I did my stretch and hustled up Turk Street.

I felt better than alive. For the moment, the sky was clear and streaked with pink and the slumbering city seemed at peace. Today, December 31, meant I had made it through another year. I'd always looked forward to the New Year and all the possibilities it brought. I believed I had made some progress in sorting out that Norman Appliances mess, and I felt optimistic about things in general: Lloyd Norman, Lowell's issues with me, even Aja's recent visit. I was alive and fit, still a handsome man and a kid at heart, eager for all that awaited me in life. Cody and Ophelia had indicated wanting to invite me to a New Year's Eve party, and maybe they would. Maybe I would accept it, too. I slowed my jog down to a walk and went back home.

I showered and dressed in my T-shirt and Levi's, high as a motherfucker from the endorphins swimming around in my brain. You drive your body hard enough through strenuous physical exercise, and the reward you get, aside from a healthy heart and a tight butt, is a chemical rush only junkies know about.

I had at least an hour to myself before I had to make some phone calls, so I fixed myself a bowl of Wheaties and read the *Chronicle* online while I drank a couple of cups of coffee. Aja's harmonica sat in one corner of my microloft. I tried not to look at it because it reminded me that she was back in town and I was a damn fool to do her any favors.

Mercedes called me from Mutual. "Cool, I checked out Vince's office. Nothing there."

"Damn."

"Maybe he's got something incriminating in the trunk of his car," she said.

"If it's there, how would we get it?"

"You tell me. You're the expert on breaking and entering."

"Well," I said, "best thing right now is for you to look alive over there and see what you can find out. I'm pretty sure that Vince has something to do with that Norman Appliances shit. I wonder who he knows over there. Have you checked through his

Rolodex?"

"He's known the top people over there for years. He used to write their policies, so, knowing Vince, I would say he's memorized their numbers. But I'll check his Rolo anyway. Gotta go."

Click.

At eight, I tried to call Brandy Capwell in Chicago, but her roomie answered and said that Brandy had flown out to California or somewhere. I asked her to relay the message that I wanted her to contact me.

I called TSX, the credit agency, but they told me that my friend had the day off, and she was the only one there who would help me. I started to get the impression that today, New Year's Eve day, would be slow and frustrating for me.

Ophelia called a little later to say they were having people over for drinks, and would I care to join them?

"I'll be there." I didn't like to sound like I had nothing else going on, but the fact was, I didn't want to spend this New Year's Eve playing with myself. Worse, I didn't want Aja coming by, asking, "Hey, baby, want some company?"

"Anything I can help with?" I asked Ophelia. "A bottle of wine?"

"As a matter of fact, I have a huge amount of cleanup work to do, and there are only three of us— me, myself and I. I sure could use a strong man's help moving a few things."

"What time?"

"How about four-thirty?"

"Done."

"Good. I should be back from shopping by then. Allison will be here around five and she'll get busy with us. The others will show up at around seven.

We'll party till the food and booze are gone." She paused. "You should wear that Versace I gave you. I'd love to know how it fits."

"Whatever you say."

I called Lloyd Norman. I didn't want to call him or talk to him, but I needed to hear what he had to say about Huey Capwell. Amazingly, he took my call. I told him about what I had learned and asked him about it. He said nothing for the longest time, so finally I said, "You there?"

"Yeah." His breathing was audible. "Cool, I can't deal with this. I don't what you want me to say. After he died, I know that Brandy thought *I* had something to do with it. She didn't exactly say, 'Lloyd Norman is a murderer,' but she sure seemed to think I was. Did I kill him? No, no, no. Can I prove my innocence? No, I can't. All I can say is, 'Why would I want to kill him?'"

"Wasn't he thinking of jumping ship and starting up his own company?"

"Oh, he *talked* about it, but saying it and doing it are two different things. He got mad once and tried to resign, but my father called him in and they had a nice long talk. Huey ended up with a raise and promotion to V.P."

"When did all that happen?"

"Not long before his death."

"For real? Didn't you think that was strange?"

"Yeah. Brandy was saying, 'It was murder, not suicide.' I agreed with her. Huey was upbeat and full of life, not some morose, sad guy who kept saying, 'What is the point of living?' Plus, my dad had just given him a big raise and promotion. But there's Brandy, flipping out, saying, 'Lloyd Norman killed my husband!' Go figure people."

"Just wondering: Has Mutual of Northern California contacted you lately?"

He paused, the spoke slowly "Yesterday they called. They're giving their Norman file to the police."

Shitfuck. "How much information does the file contain?"

He now spoke faster and more quietly. "Wrong time and place for this conversation. Let's do it in private, OK?"

"Yeah. I'm going to Ophelia's party tonight. We'll rap then." I had no desire to hang out with him, at his sister's mansion or anywhere else, but he probably had shit to say that I needed to hear. Besides, I really had nothing to lose. I seemed to be a conspiracy suspect, and that sucked balls. I had dealt with criminals for most of my adult life, but I wasn't one myself and didn't like being treated as one. The whole mess was making me feel anxious and ill, and I needed a distraction.

I went to Market Street and bought a pair of shiny black Florsheims. I'm not much for shopping, but the experience filled with me with excitement for the social event that evening. I had to remind myself that once in a while, I liked to put on some fresh clothes and party—even if it's with rich white people I've only just met. I started feeling sorry for Cody and Ophelia, who, just yesterday, seemed so profligate and decadent. They were who they were, and I had no business judging them. It was up to her, where she went and what she did. If her thing was to play tennis and buy clothes…well, what of it? She did some charity work, which was more than I ever did. Ophelia said that the bad things in this world were done by those who felt cast away and pushed aside. Yes. As a cop, I had met many criminals, and the worst of them were lonely, bored people who could not find an entry point into human society. Complacent people don't murder, rape and rob.

For a few moments I thought of getting my sweats together and going to the gym. Then I thought, Why do that? So I stayed in and turned on the TV set. I watched CNN for a few hours. I nodded off, woke up and watched CNN some more. Why do they keep recycling their stories?

At about three o'clock, I squeezed into my pitiful excuse for a shower and scrubbed for close to half an hour. Then I toweled off and tried on Cody's Versace suit. It fit perfectly, including the tie and dress shirt. I knew very little about being a gentleman in a designer suit. My folks died when I was a kid, and my aunt who raised me cared more about daily survival than teaching little Coolidge about how to be a man, not that she would have known. I knew lots about being a wild little boy who tagged everything in sight with spray paint. By my teens I had started hanging out with local punks who talked trash and smoked weed. I was too afraid of guns and blood (especially my own) to join the Bloods or Crips, and deep down inside I believed my aunt's admonition: Crime don't pay. By the time I came of age, I had straightened out and joined the Army, then the P.D. Now I'm a law-abiding citizen most of the time. At the core, I'm upright and uptight. Being a private investigator allows me to be naughty and nosy and get away with it.

By four-thirty, I was standing at the Terrymans' front door, ringing their bell and hearing its chime through the door. I looked through the window and thought the house was empty. Their mailbox stood bursting with envelopes, and a shoebox-sized parcel sat on the front porch next to the mailbox. Their Siamese cat wandered by, checked me out for a minute and decided I wasn't worth his time.

Then I saw their gate swing open and a maroon Bentley roll in. Ophelia smiled and waved from behind the steering wheel. She got out and I went up to her.

"Lemme help you with all that," I said.

"Please do. I'm afraid I'm a little late. Did I keep you waiting long?"

"Just got here myself."

I took a couple of bags and she took one. I could see some others in the trunk and back seat.

"Cody is right behind me. He has all the booze," she said.

"How many people are you expecting?"

"A few dozen," she said. "Let's get these bags in and let Cody worry about the others. We have lots of work to do."

We hurried towards the front door. Behind me, I heard the purr of an engine and the crunch of gravel as Cody entered in his silver Rolls Royce. Nice cars, I thought. Must be fun to have such toys.

At the door, Ophelia said, "Here, take one of these bags so I can get this parcel."

I did as told, and she somehow got the parcel into the crook of her left arm. "Jeez, it's a heavy sucker," she said, breathing hard.

The cat came by again, sniffing and mewing. Cody parked his car and began unloading the liquor bottles from his trunk. Ophelia wrestled the door open and practically stumbled inside, and the phone began to ring. She heaved the parcel onto the hall table.

It happened so fast that I didn't have time to react. It started with a round flash of light that made me feel as if the whole world had turned white, followed by an explosion of sound too loud to be heard. The light turned into a gray cloud from which shards of metal sprang out as if fired from a gun. Then a fireball, not unlike a sphere of metal shot from a cannon, rolled outside and charred the grass as it traveled past.

I felt myself being lifted, as by a hundred crazy men, and flung onto the front lawn, slamming into a broad, leafy tree, my back sore and new shoes now gone. I saw Ophelia fly past me, as comical and ridiculous as a cartoon character, smashing against the hedge and crumpling in a heap on the ground, a store-bought princess broken in half. I blinked away some of the lights, shook my head to clear it of disbelief, but my heart thundered and ears buzzed. I sniffed and cringed at the smell of gunpowder.

In the Army I had seen men, women and children shot dead, dismembered by bombs, their limbs and skulls blown off in chunks and slivers. Hollywood will never be able to replicate such an event, because the *smell* of death is much of what makes it so vile. For an insane moment I envied Ophelia, for she was surely dead by the time she hit the ground.

I saw with disbelief that the whole front of the house had been blown away, much like the disaster areas I had attended as a police officer. But on those occasions I had not known the victims, much less been one. I felt too confused to be afraid or surprised. I had absolutely no idea what had just happened, only that something somewhere had blown up. Only later did I learn that the wrapped box on the doorstep had been a bomb.

Very soon I figured out that I had been injured. My eyebrows had been singed; blood dripped from my ears. Then the pain began, worse than any agony I could ever recall. I looked over at Cody, sitting on the lawn in his cocktail outfit, his bloody but his eyes focused as he frowned at me. Ophelia was dead, but Cody seemed alive, even OK, and for a moment I thought he would be strong enough to get up and ask me to help him do whatever he thought you did immediately after someone bombed your house. Don't sweat it, Cody, I wanted to say. I'm comfy as can be against this tree. Looks like the Versace suit you gave me is shit now, and where the *fuck* are my shoes?

I closed my eyes and felt ready for sleep, not altogether sure of where I was or why. When I opened them again, I saw many bemused faces staring at me. Those people wore uniforms and slickers. I looked up past them and saw that the house was on fire. People said shit to me, but I couldn't hear a thing, I just saw talking heads. They were funny; I giggled.

The chaos continued for a little while before men in white shirts pulled me away from the tree and onto a stretcher. I didn't fight them as they took me away. I started to feel ill but didn't want to barf all over myself. And I wanted them to put a few dozen more blankets on me—I felt *so* cold.

IT'S ALL GOOD

15

Before long, my hearing came back and I started remembering things. I looked up and saw Aja standing over me, and I could have sworn I saw a momentary flicker of concern in her eyes. But no; Aja had never given a fuck about anybody but Number One. Right next to her stood a nursie. I wished Aja would go away and let the nursie do her thing. I moved my lips and she leaned in.

"I think he's waking up," she said, and the nursie disappeared. "What is it, baby? You hurtin' bad? Want some meds?"

I said, "You cunt," but wasn't sure if she heard me

right. Didn't mean shit to her, anyway; she just laughed at people's insults. I promised myself to recover as fast as I could and then tell her to fuck off forever. Then I shut my eyes and tried to sleep.

I couldn't sleep. I could only think of the explosion—the round white light, the impossibly loud *bang!* and the energy that sent us, literally, flying into the front yard and ravaged so much of that house.

I pictured Ophelia, flying over me, freakish and contorted, looking like a Barbie doll that had been flung away by a child in a fit of temper. She was dead; what about Cody? I glanced at Aja, wondering if she knew.

She seemed to know what I wanted. "You're OK, Cool. You're in the hospital, and so is Cody." She paused. "Ophelia—"

I shook my head and looked away, wishing Aja would give me some time to myself.

I closed my eyes and asked myself, *Where does it hurt?* It hurt in many places. I love most of me, and the parts I don't love, I really like a lot. I felt the way I did because of bruises, whiplash, an IV needle, pain meds and pressure dressings on my burns. Even though I had been standing so close to Ophelia when the boom went down and she went ass over promises across her front lawn, my own injuries—contusions and abrasions, a mild concussion, superficial burns and shock—had been minor. Lucky me.

I had a few dozen questions about that cocktail party that turned into such a blast, literally, even before it got started, but I had figured out a thing or two already. I remembered that shoebox-sized package that Ophelia said was so heavy; clearly, it contained a bomb powerful enough to destroy lives and property. Who had put it there? I wanted to rip out my IV, get out of that hospital and start finding out what the fuck was going on.

The doctor came in, a black woman in her fifties with a soft, kindly face. I liked her because she asked Aja to leave the room without ogling her first. I watched as she checked my vital signs. *Am I gonna be OK, Mama?* Her not particularly well-tended Afro do was half gray. I thought she could pass for Morgan Freeman's unglamorous daughter. She gave my hand the longest squeeze and asked, "You hangin' in there, big man?" as if she really wanted an answer, so I nodded.

I teared up a little bit. I looked up at that doctor and saw my mother instead, and I felt three years old again, lying there with a boo-boo that needed no medical attention except Mama's. I had never really allowed myself to experience the warmth and tenderness radiated by those in the healing arts. Maybe that was because I hated the feeling of helplessness and I *really* hated anyone's pity, especially my own. I was my own man and I could make my own way through life and I had my own back, thank you very much. Still, I liked being in that hospital, too banged up to look after myself, grateful to be looked after for the time being.

Soon she was nearly finished with me, and I felt more together, eager to figure out when I would feel well enough to resume my life.

She said I was in a private room at Memorial. The paramedics had brought in me through the ER. I nodded and told her I remembered the sirens and lights, the smoke and other smells, the rush to the hospital and the controlled madness of the ER. I recalled smiling as they stripped me of my sooty, smelly Versace original, cleaned me up and put me into bed. I lay there, shot full of dope and ready to snooze. When I woke up, I saw that the clock said nine in the morning, but the effort of looking at the clock and figuring out the time was just too much effort, and I conked out again. I felt muzzy and wanted them to shut off my dope so I could think straight and stay awake.

At some point they removed my IV and a nursie's aide helped me to the bathroom and cleaned me up, then adjusted my bed so I could it up and revisit the world, sort of. By then the clock said it was nearly noon, and I thought back with much regret about the platefuls of *hors d'oeuvres* I'd missed out on the night before because of that shoebox bomb. No wonder I was so ravenous now! The nursie's aide found me a tuna sandwich from somewhere and I devoured it in three bites. Aja had surely gone to the hospital cafeteria for lunch, so I requested a NO VISITORS sign on my door.

Lieutenant Lando must not have seen the sign, because when I came out of one of my naps, I saw him sitting in my room, his face in a magazine. He is a big human being, tall and broad across, with jowls and a paunch. His silvery hair is thin and he buys the cheapest slacks and sports coats in town. Maybe he had partied too hard the night before and expected to watch football games on TV instead of being there with me.

I shifted a little bit and he saw me. "Coolidge?"

"Lieutenant." We'd known each other for years, and he'd never forgiven me for retiring from the PD to become a private dick. A cop's cop, he runs the

Homicide Division of the San Francisco Police Department and had considered me one of the PD's rising stars until, as he might have put it, I pissed it all way for private-dick work. He doesn't like what I do for a living and I get sick and tired of having to explain to him and the other coppers that I have a right to ask them questions and get straight answers. Anyway, I didn't like homicide cases, which always meant dealing with Lando. If I could avoid such work, I would do so.

"You up to talking?" he asked.

"No," I said, "but ask and I'll answer."

He got up and came over. I had no backtalk for him from my hospital bed, and he probably felt disappointed. "Tell me what happened."

"Ophelia and I gathered up grocery bags. There was a shoebox wrapped in brown paper on the front step. She picked it up, as if it was some kind of present. She half-threw it onto the table and *kaboom!*"

He nodded. "Not much left of her. You made it through OK, considering how close you were to the action. Cody got banged up a bit. He says he remembers nothing, but he will."

"Bomb," I said. "Not too many of those in this country. I hear bomb, I think of Belfast or Gaza."

He shrugged. "Package wrapped in brown paper? No UPS delivery? No signature? You just come home and find it there and don't wonder why it's there or who sent it? Strike you as weird, Coolidge?"

I shook my head. "It was there, she picked it up. I assumed she knew what it was." My mind was getting sharp and fast. I wanted to get my ass out of there and solve this fuckin' case.

"The oldest question in the book, Coolidge. Do

you know offhand of anyone who might have wanted to harm the Terrymans? Did either of them say anything to you?"

I flashed back to my glass of wine at O'Hare with Brandy Capwell, and my conversation with Cody. I nearly laughed at the fear in his face as that big man told me that wimpy little Brandy had threatened him over the phone.

I told Lando all about it. "Cody told me that Brandy said something like, 'You just never know when you're gonna die.' She thinks Lloyd killed Huey, so why is she threatening Cody?"

Lando wrote it all down in that sort of shorthand only he could read. I told him everything I knew, and actually felt good about sharing it with him. Bombs and murder threats? Shit, I couldn't deal with that. Time to call in the PD. Only thing was, Lando, like all other cops, listened and wrote it all down, but gave me back zero. He would say, "I don't know," but he was thinking plenty and refused to share his thoughts.

"So is your suspicion that Brandy Capwell is back in town?" he asked me.

"That's what I'm coming up with. Cody's a patient here too, right?"

Lando nodded. "Other end of the ward."

"Good idea if I went over and said hidy?"

"Absolutely. He'd be grateful for the company."

Soon Lando left and I swung my legs over the side of the bed. It hurt just to do that much, and I noticed for the first time how discolored my body was from my recent trauma. I tried to stand but my legs wobbled, as if to say, *No can do, baby.* So I sat there and cussed out the dickless piece of shit who'd put that bomb on the Terrymans' front porch.

I heard a knock on the door. The nursie stuck her head in. "Your wife is here to see you. She says she has to go but she wants a minute with you anyway.

"I have no wife," I said.

"Well, whoever she is, she seems very concerned about you. She's been here all night, you know."

The nursie saw how much trouble I was having getting comfortable in bed, so she helped me out. She looked about twenty-five, a fresh-faced and caring young thing, not yet burned out from too many cranky patients and filthy bedpans. I was not much older than this woman when I married Aja, and a year older when Aja took off. No explanation, no heart-to-heart rap concerning how she felt about where we were and how we could be better. Our no-fault divorce happened so fast that I could scarcely believe she and I were over and that I was a again an unmarried man, free to fuck whomever I chose, as she had done during our marriage.

I snapped my fingers and said, "I need a wheelchair. There's someone here I want to visit. Mister Terryman."

She nodded. "He's at the other end of the ward."

"He survived the bomb blast too, huh?"

"Oh, sure. He's going home this afternoon."

"The police officer investigating the blast thinks I should go over and say hello to Mister Terryman."

"And your wife—?"

"Ain't got one. But send her in anyway. Try to find me a wheelchair, OK? I want to see Mister Terryman, but if I try to walk that far, I'll fall on my fine black ass sue everyone in sight."

She must not have wanted to hear about my fanny or lawsuits, because she left without another word.

My wife. Fuck *that* nonsense.

16

She looked exhausted, as if she'd spent the entire night trying to sleep on a chair or two in the waiting room. She held a hand over her mouth as she yawned, and then she stretched. Her T-shirt rode up over her tummy, which was impossibly ripped and tight. Some people just never gain weight.

"Doctor says she won't sign your discharge order until she knows you have some to look after you at home," Aja told me.

"Uh-uh. I can do OK by myself."

"Doctor *said*."

"But not to me."

"She probably did, but you don't remember because you were all doped up," Aja said.

"That bullshit. I hate this place. I'm going home."

She nodded. "Yeah, that's what I told her. I just think you should know that I want to help you. I can ask the doc to sign your discharge order and then I can take you home. I don't have to stay there with you—that place is *way* too small, Coolidge! How come you such a puny place? And in the *Tenderloin*! Ain't you got no sense at all? Look, I take you home and check on you twice a day, in case you need. And you *will* need help."

"Lemme think about it." But she was right: With Emma, Orlanda and Roberta all out of town for now, I had nobody to impose on. And I knew I couldn't cope all by myself, not yet. I suddenly knew the despair experienced by crazy people, retarded people and crippled people whenever they tried to do even the simplest things. They were just too debilitated. I couldn't make it at home, and I couldn't make it at the hospital. The hospital was as bad as my home. Worse, maybe. The docs and nursies are in too much of a hurry and they make mistakes. A person could die in there. Many people did.

Aja bent down and kissed the tip of my nose. "Think about my offer. I'll be back soon."

Poof. She was gone.

When the nursie came in, I asked, "Is it OK for me to visit Mister Terryman?"

"Why sure."

"I'll need a wheelchair."

"I'll get you one." Half an hour later, she did just that. As I sat alone on my hospital bed, I admitted that I had fallen into a depression despite having convinced myself that I was immune to mental illness. Ophelia's death had brought on these feelings for me. We hadn't been friends, and just barely acquaintances, but she had been a minor character in the movie of my life. I had first met her back in high school, when Allison had acquired my friendship as one might procure an exotic new living pet that does not particularly wish to be regarded as someone else's property. Ophelia left our school in her junior year, and I didn't see her anymore but heard things: She had enrolled in a boarding school in Connecticut or Massachusetts; she was skiing in Switzerland or Utah (maybe both). Her family had the means to let her do as she pleased, hoping, perhaps, that she would find a purpose in life and, thus, "find herself." I was ashamed to admit that I cared as little about her as I assumed she did me, and for as long as I had known Allison, every time I met Ophelia we said little more than hello and goodbye. Now she had been killed, like a patsy, finding an anonymous parcel and unintentionally detonating it the way soldiers in Iraq routinely encountered explosive devices disguised as toys. I blamed myself, too, for being a fool and not recognizing that parcel as something suspicious. How long had I been a soldier or cop, anyway? Why hadn't I been hip right away to the possible dangers of spending an evening with Cody and Ophelia, with the Norman fire scandal and Brandy Capwell's freaky phone call to Cody?

Once in my wheelchair, I rolled my way to the other end of the ward to see Cody. They had closed the door and Brynne stood next to it, his arms folded. When he saw me, he turned to face me. She had the dark, gaunt beauty of a runway model, and saw something very chic in the slightly disheveled way she wore her clothes, as if she had just thrown them on. I supposed that was the point. That was Brynne's look.

"Hey, Brynne, I'm Coolidge Jones. We've met a few times over the years."

She ran a hand through her thick, dark, beautiful messy hair. "Oh, sure. You're Allison's friend from school." She bent down and gave me an air kiss. The prettiest of the Norman sisters, Brynne had wide-set hazel eyes, a small, straight nose and a big, toothy, irresistible smile, much like Aja's. They told me that Brynne wanted to become a pop star and had spent a dozen years in several cities trying to fulfill her ambition. She certainly had the looks to hold an audience's attention, and she hardly needed a great voice or a surfeit of musical talent to make it big in popular music. Maybe, as her family said, she'd been too busy smoking crack or getting laid to commit herself to music. I didn't know.

"I want to go in and see Cody," I told her.

She nodded. "They're fixing him up a little bit. The doctor is ready to sign his discharge order. Are you OK? They said you were here, too, and you're in a wheelchair…"

I waved her off. "I'll survive. I'm sorry about Ophelia."

She nodded her thanks. "A bomb on our doorstep? That's too much. I didn't know the Taliban was after us."

"It must be hard on your mother."

"She's been through plenty in her life. She just knows how to cope. It's very difficult for her. Allison is a mess. She and Ophelia were so tight." She looked at me some more. "You sure you're OK?"

"I got banged up a little and the meds are starting to fade. Not one of my better days."

"They tell me you got off lucky," she said.

"I don't feel lucky. I remember looking at that parcel and thinking that it was weird: No UPS or FedEx labels on it or postage stamps. I should have considered it a very suspicious item. By the way, are you staying at your mother's house?"

"Yes. I flew in and Ophelia called and said, 'We're having a New Year's Eve party. Wanna come?' And I'm like, 'Yeah, sounds like fun.' I went swimming in the afternoon and Edina came running out—she never runs for *nobody*—and she looks like she's just seen a ghost. She's the total control freak, right? So I'm wondering what's got her tripping out like this. I pull myself out of the pool and said, 'What's up?' and she says, 'A bomb just went off at Ophelia's. She's dead.' Ophelia is hyperventilating and I'm laughing because someone's gotta be a practical joke on her. Houses just don't get bombed, you know what I'm saying? So I'm standing there laughing and Edina's face goes from white to red. He hauls off and backhands me across the face and screams, *'Bitch! I'm serious!'* Now I'm full of questions but Cody says he doesn't remember shit and the cops say, 'No comment.'"

I ran it down for her. Brynne's expressions ranged from bemusement to moderate anger and back to bemusement. She was telling the truth; nobody had said much to her about how Ophelia had died.

"So we have far more questions than answers," she said.

"Ain't that always the way."

"I think Allison was on her way to Ophelia's to

help with the party when the bomb exploded," said Brynne. "As soon as Edina was finished slapping the taste out of my mouth, she said, 'Get dressed! We need to go to her!' So we did. By the time we got there, the paramedics were putting Cody into the ambulance and they had put a white sheet over Ophelia. You were on a stretcher, too, muttering to yourself. I don't know what you were saying."

"Just my usual bullshit," I told her.

She nodded without a smile. I thought Brynne had missed her calling—she belonged in TV news, not popular music. She spoke of her family's very recent tragedy with the calmest, most straightforward detachment.

I thought for a moment and pictured Brynne at the crime scene, hers just one of the faces peering down at me as I lay on the stretcher. By then, shock had reduced me to a blabbering fool, and my teeth kept chattering despite the intense of the fire and the blankets they had put on me. I don't think I saw Edina; maybe the cops kept her out because her sister lay there, entire pieces of her ripped from her body and leaning against the wall, like hunks of bloody, bony meat, a meal for wild dogs.

I rested my chin on my hand and let out a huge, morose sigh. Brynne twitched, as if wanting to console me with a touch or pat but unsure of where to put her hand. She probably just wanted to keep her hands to herself and get her ass *out of there*. If so, that made two of us.

"Cody's gonna be OK," I said.

"Yes. Couple of cracked ribs, cut face but nothing worse than that. He wants to go, too."

Cody's door finally opened, and a nursie emerged

with soiled bandages. She smelled of hospital stuff: antiseptics, gauze, adhesive tape.

"You can go in now," said the nursie. "Doctor says he can go home as soon as he wants."

Brynne went in first, and I followed her in my wheelchair. Cody sat at the edge of the bed, looking much smaller than I remembered. He seemed to be pouting or frowning, as if his feelings, more than his body, had been hurt. Maybe Ophelia's death had done that to him, but my guess was that if he loved his wife, he loved himself more. He would get over her soon enough and remarry.

Edina entered the room, and I suddenly felt claustrophobic. I needed to get out of there for a few minutes.

"I'll be right back," I said, wheeling myself out. Edina followed me right into the row of seats next to the gift shop. She sat and swallowed hard.

"This is so scary," she said, licking her lips. "Someone left a *bomb* at my sister's house? Are they out to get *her?* What has *she* done to anyone?"

I shook my head. "Not her. Him."

"Cody?"

"Yes. I remember. That parcel was addressed to him."

Edina scowled. "That makes no sense either. The cops said—"

I waved her off. "The cops don't know jackshit. I was there. I saw the parcel."

"No."

"'No'? You callin' me a liar?"

"I'm not calling anyone anything," she said. "That son of a bitch…"

I wheeled around to face her. "Edina, talk to me. I

need to know what you're thinking. Do you know who killed Ophelia?"

She gave a stern look. "If I did, I would tell you. Do you think I wouldn't?" Her face then contorted in grief and she wept for several minutes.

"Ophelia said," I told her as she blew her nose and collected herself, "that she was going to vote against you."

Edina's anger returned. "You *asshole!* Just fuck off!"

I wheeled my way back towards my room. Brynne caught up with me. "Coolidge—"

"Later." I wheeled myself right back into my room and found Mercedes waiting for me.

"Vince's quit," she told me.

17

I got back into bed as Mercedes talked.

"He came rushing into the office at about ten o'clock yesterday," she said. "Lowell said, 'We're staying open till five tonight; I don't give a rat's ass if it *is* New Year's Eve.' Well, Vince had a lunch meeting *and* a two o'clock with one of the veeps. So he's getting into this *panic*, and when I tried to give him his phone messages, he refused them and he went into his office. He started clearing it out! He put all his shit into his briefcase and split." She shook her head. "Too fucking weird. He took his Rolo, too. Maybe he knows who set the warehouse fire."

"Vince knows many things," I said. "That's why they paid him the big bucks."

"I guess. Anyway, he didn't come back, so at five I got into my car and drove out to his apartment."

"Out by the beach?"

"Yessir. I didn't like all that *attitude* he was putting out. He was really on the rag and I wanted to check that out with him. I buzzed him at the front door and when nobody answered, I buzzed the next number and said, 'I'm a friend of Vince. He's not answering.' They said, 'He's moved out, or he's moving out.'"

"Do you know if the online news services have reported much on how Ophelia Terryman was killed?"

"Not much. The cops aren't telling the media the details yet."

I suddenly felt pumped full of energy and anxiety. I threw off the covers and said, "Help me get out of here. Shit's happening. I need to get busy."

"Doctor says it's OK?"

"Yeah. Doctor says I'm happy and handsome and a delight to my friends. Check the closet and see if Aja brought me a change of clothes." That Versace suit was now in such poor shape that even the most desperate homeless person would sneer at it. Then I noticed my house keys sitting on the table. "Forget the clothes. There are my keys. Just take me home."

Mercedes frowned. "You sure?"

"Let's do it."

"Coolidge, the doctor—"

"The doctor told Aja I could go home so long as I had someone looking after me."

"Like hell."

"Mercedes, would I lie to you?"

"You've lied to me a hundred times."

I sighed. "Mercedes, just shut the fuck up and help me out of here. Patients can leave the hospital. They do it every day. Let's vacate this sick bed for someone who actually needs it."

"What about paying your bill?"

I rolled my eyes. "I have insurance. Plus, if I owe them money, they have my address. They'll send me an invoice."

She muttered "OK" and helped me back into the wheelchair. Then she pushed me out of the room and down the hallway, towards the elevators. When we encountered the nursie's aide, I smiled and tossed her a little wave. She smiled and waved back.

I still had on my hospital gown and felt sure that security or someone else would stop me. But no; Mercedes wheeled me to her car, I got in and closed the door. She put the wheelchair aside and got into her car. Fuck hospitals and being sick! I had places to go, things to do, bad guys to take down.

We made good time; by just after three I was back home, feeling as if I had away for weeks instead of just one day. "You don't look so good," Mercedes said as I stumbled about.

"I gotta get dressed," I said.

"You want me to wait outside?"

"What for? I ain't got nothin' you've never seen before." A moment later, I stood butt-naked before her. "See anything you like?"

"Nice cock," she said.

"What, this ol' thang?" I tugged at my johnson.

Then I sat on my bed and pulled on my Jockeys and Levi's. "Let's go to Mutual and see if Vince left anything we can use." Then I put on a sweatshirt and went into the bathroom to brush my teeth and gargle. In the mirror, I saw a black man who had been out in the sun for too long. Aside from that, I looked like the same Cool. Nice for me.

I took the file folder I had stolen out of Vince's apartment, then put on thick white socks and sneakers, and finally my leather jacket. San Francisco is a notorious cold, windy, foggy city at night.

Outside, with the car's windows down, I thought it seemed more like summer than January. The sky, at least for the moment, was baby blue and just a few clouds scudded by. Not much of a breeze, either. I looked around and couldn't find Aja or her piece-of-shit car, which made me feel better. If she'd been with me, she just would have started ragging on me about my premature return from the hospital. I'd noticed that my battered Ford was in the carport, where it belonged. I needed to find out who did that and thank them.

Mercedes drove us to Mutual. We encountered zero traffic through the heart of downtown because of the major holiday. Mutual's carport sat empty, too.

We used the back entrance. "You want to know what's really bugging the hell out of me about all this?" I asked Mercedes as we stood at the elevator.

"Tell me."

"Well, we're assuming that Vince is guilty of conspiracy to commit insurance fraud even though we really don't have any proof. So or no?"

"So," she said as we entered the elevator.

"Well, I'm thinking, if he *did* get involved in all this, how come? If he gets busted, it's a felony and his ass is had. So why does he do it?"

She shrugged. "Payoff. He gets his cut. I know

that Noelle really shook him down in divorce court, so he needs cash."

"That's the problem. Someone knew him well enough to say, 'Hey, Vince, let's do a scam on Mutual and get some easy money.' Vince's been in the insurance business for a long time. He's seen his share of fraudulent claims and he's seen the bad guys get busted. So why does *he* become a bad guy? I don't like him but I've never thought of him as an idiot or criminal."

The big, immaculate elevator slowed and stopped. The doors opened and we stepped out. We sauntered over to Mutual's big, immaculate glass doors, and Mercedes let us in with her keys. Inside, she turned on the lights and put her handbag on a table.

"So…?" she asked, looking at me.

"So I'm wondering if there are big things going on with this case that I don't yet know about. Vince had full access to the claim files. He could fuck with them and alter them, but that's illegal as hell and he could face serious charges. Then he freaks out. He panics. Why?"

"Ophelia's house was bombed. She got killed. That must have contributed to Vince's freakout."

We entered Vince's office and Mercedes said, "I'll stand here, you search."

I took my time and started with his business files. Everything seemed to be in place; of course, this was the computer age, and his files were mostly stored in Mutual's network. I tapped on his IBM desktop and said, "Sure wish we had his password. Then we could really check him out."

"Well, we don't," Mercedes said.

"Yeah, and if he had any naughty or nasty or

incriminating files, I doubt he would have them on Mutual's network. That's the first place the IRS or FBI would look." I plopped down into his big leather swivel chair and looked around. "You know what? I wish I could crawl inside his head. Where did he go and why did he take off the way he did?"

"Search me, man," Mercedes said, still standing against the office door.

"Do you know Noelle's number?"

"I can get it. You want me to call her and find out if she knows where he's gone?"

I nodded. "Make up some bullshit reason for calling. Find out what *she* knows but be sure you don't tell her what *we* know."

"I hear ya." Mercedes left the office to go to her own desk to get Noelle's number and pump her for information. I picked up the file I had brought and went through its contents. Vince certainly seemed to be in deep financial ca-ca. Noelle had her boot up his butt about late payments and other folks wanted theirs, too. He had a fancy appointment book he'd taken with him and a calendar pad he'd left behind. "When he leaves his office during business hours he jots things down so we'll know where he is and when," Mercedes had told me. "I guess he forgets that he has a cell phone and we have his number, and that's how we keep track of his whereabouts. We just call him and ask, 'Vince, where are you?'"

On his calendar pad, he'd circled nine at night on Christmas Eve and written "R." I thought at first that such initials might belong to his girlfriend. I checked earlier dates and found the same initials here and there. I gathered up some of the paperwork and went over to Mercedes.

"Yes, ma'am," she was saying. "I understand your feelings. I wouldn't like it, either. What has your lawyer told you? Well, you should take your lawyer's advice very seriously. I mean, that's why lawyers are here, right? Look, Noelle, I have to hang up now. I'm in the middle of some very serious business of my own. I'm hanging up now, Noelle. Bye." Click.

She rolled her eyes. "That woman needs a shrink, or at least a best friend she can bitch to, and I ain't gonna be that girl."

"Give you anything?" I asked.

"She said she's pissed at Vince because he didn't pick up the kids last night like he was supposed to. She had her own plans and had to call off her own good time because of him. She's ready to call the police because she thinks he's left town."

I shook my head. "The cops will just tell her that the person has to be missing for seventy-two hours before they'll get involved. He's probably banging his girlfriend as we speak. Here, let me show you one of his love letters."

Mercedes read it, her lips curling over each word. "Yuck! What a pervert! What's this part say, anyway?" She held it up to me.

"You're better off not knowing."

She shrugged. "I guess. He must have a fetish for big zoomers."

"So do I."

"Maybe that's why he's never liked me," Mercedes said. "My titties aren't big enough."

"Be grateful he didn't like you. If he had liked you, he wouldn't have kept trying to get in your pants."

"Don't make me gag." Then, "Enough about big fat Vince and his flabby little cock. What else did you find out about him and the fire and everything else?"

"Got this calendar pad with 'R' on it in places. Not sure what it means, but maybe 'R' is the other woman."

"I wonder if she's ever called him on his office line," Mercedes said. "I can check that out. Our computers keep track of those things. We're trying to be high-tech around here, you know." She logged in and soon came up with at least one repeat number to Vince's office line.

We went online to do a reverse-number lookup and discovered that this one was up the hill on Taylor Street, not far from my Tenderloin microloft but in a much better neighborhood. Renee Brooks lived there.

"Renee," I said, "Cool's on the way."

"Should you be doing that?" Mercedes asked. "You don't look so good. You need rest and food."

"I'll chow down and snooze after I see Renee." But Mercedes was right—I needed to chill. First, however, I wanted to get some A's or my Q's. I was running on pure adrenalin, which was a fine drug as long as it lasted. Once it faded, I were fucked, but I didn't feel fucked yet, so I went to see Renee.

18

Mercedes agreed to drop me off on Taylor Street and then go her own way. I would interview Renee, and wanted to do it by myself. That's my preferred way whenever I'm trying to extract information from someone I've never met. For me, one-on-one is easier because I don't have to worry about what my co-interviewer might say, and I'm free to lie, threaten or cajole the interviewee. Not to brag, but I'm a big, mean-looking black dude with a deep, loud voice. I can get people to tell me what I need to know.

The apartment building was boxy and faded pink,

one of those ancient, plaster-and-wood structures that miraculously wasn't pancaked during the last earthquake. Like so many other buildings in San Francisco, this one had an iron gate keeping out those lacking a key. However, the maintenance men had left the gate wide open, and I walked right in without being questioned by anyone or looked at the wrong way.

I knocked on the door of apartment E, wondering if Vince would answer. I couldn't imagine what I would say to him. I could smell someone's dinner cooking—chicken, garlic and onions. I felt very hungry, too. I wished whoever was frying up that tasty shit would come outside and say, "You hungry, Cool? Come on in!" Just then, the door I'd knocked on opened and I stepped back, my heart pounding.

"Noelle…?"

She shook her head. "I'm Renee, her sister."

I nodded. Her voice sounded nothing like Noelle's, and she didn't look *that* much like her sister, either. Renee was seriously into her forties and her beauty—she *had* been beautiful, that was obvious— was starting to fade in major ways. She had Noelle's shiny dark hair and dark blue eyes, but her features were finer, her chin less pointed. Both women were tall, with big breasts and long, thick muscles. Despite their big open smiles, their faces held a certain hardened wisdom, a kind of meanness, as if they had been denied the right to grow up as sweet, silly little girls. I wondered for a moment why Noelle had married a fat slob like Vince Stanich. She probably would have been happier on the back of Sonny Barger's Harley.

Vince must have loved this shit. He got both

sisters. He fell in love, if that's what it was, with Noelle because she was a sexy, busty tigress he'd wanted to tame. They had money in common: He loved to earn it and she loved to spend it. She doubtless got off on his adoration of her as well. From his letter, I got the idea she was a carnal contortionist, doing his bone and balls till he screamed for her to stop. Lucky guy.

"Is Vince here?" I asked her.

She frowned. "Vince who?"

"Vince Stanich, Noelle's husband. He and I work together at Mutual."

Renee shrugged. "I don't know where he is. Maybe my sister doesn't, either. They've called it quits, you know."

"Well, he gave me your address in case we needed to reach him."

She arched a don't-bullshit-me eyebrow. "Did he?"

"Yes, ma'am. That's why I'm here."

"Do you know my sister?"

"Not very well. I know her through Vince. When you opened the door, I thought you were Noelle. You two could be twins."

She smiled. Chalk one up for Cool.

"What do you want with Vince?" she asked.

"He disappeared yesterday. He won't answer his cell phone. We're afraid something might have happened to him. Has he been in contact with you latcly?"

"Nope."

"OK if I come in for a moment? Won't take long."

She sighed and nodded. "OK, I suppose. Vince didn't tell me he had given *my* address to anyone."

I went in, had the quickest look around and

nodded my approval. In truth, I thought this one-bedroom place was almost as big a ripoff as my microloft. She had a puny living room with a few pieces of Ikea furniture and her bedroom was probably the size of a closet. But her location was vastly superior to mine; outside, men didn't piss on her building (often).

Renee turned off her TV and motioned for me to sit in an Ikea seat and she did the same across the room. She wore a white T-shirt and khaki shorts. Nice legs, or used to be. She reminded me of a TV actress, so young fine once upon a time, and when I see her now I can sort of see the glamorous beauty she used to be and why I loved stroking my young woody as I thought of her.

"Now," she said, throwing one leg over the other, "did you say you work for Vince?"

"No, we both work for Mutual. When did you last see him?"

"I spoke to him on the phone on Thursday night. He was going somewhere with his kids on New Year's Eve so Noelle could party. Our agreement was to see each other the next morning, but he was very dependable about calling. *Very* dependable. So when I didn't hear from him at all, I drove to his apartment and he wasn't there." She paused. "Say, why would you need to contact him on New Year's Day?"

I lied to her as little as possible, telling her that he had gone on Friday morning and made himself quite unavailable. "There's a file we need from him. Did you hear about that big warehouse fire out in Oakland last month? Well, it has a lot to do with that."

Renee narrowed her eyes; she furrowed her brow. "You said your name was…?"

"Chris Dodd," I said, using the name of one of my neighbors. "I work in the office with Vince. He may have spoken to me about you once or twice on the phone."

"Well…*Chris*…Vince doesn't tell me much about his work. Just that he loves his job and does it well."

"Yes, ma'am," I said, Uncle Tomming it. "We like him just fine, and that's why we're concerned about him right now."

"I don't know what to tell you," she said, toying with the hem of her shorts and looking away from me.

I had the feeling she *did* know what to tell me but was keeping it to herself for now.

"As I say, Chris, I don't know what's going on with Vince unless he tells me. But if you're trying to find him and help him, let me know what you find out. I don't like just sitting here and wondering if something awful has happened to him."

"I appreciate your concern. I'll keep you posted on what's going on." I wrote down my iPhone number and handed it to her.

"I hope he's all right," she muttered, sounding sincere for the first time during our conversation.

"I'm sure he is." In truth, I believed he was scared shitless and had run away from his troubles.

Renee took a few minutes to stare at my ravaged face. "Don't mind, but are *you* OK?"

I chuckled. "Oh, I just hurt myself shaving." She smirked at my fib, then looked some more at my face and tsked. "I'll keep looking for Vince and I'll let you know what's happening," I repeated.

I left her building and my evening went downhill, literally. Renee lived most of the way up three steep hills, I lived in the Tenderloin, at the bottom of those hills. I walked downhill and got winded anyway. I cursed myself for leaving the hospital. Now that I had to care for myself, I thought of how fine it would be to lie between the hospital's crisp white sheets and let the nursies burp me. Instead, I ached all over and my pretty face felt singed. For dinner I would have fast food or canned crap.

I stopped and scowled at the sight of Aja's battered ride parked on Turk Street. I looked inside. Nobody home. I turned the corner and there she was, leaning against the parking lot gate, looking finer than anyone had a right to. "I missed you," she said.

"You shouldn't stand there like that," I told her. "People might think you're a ho."

She shrugged. "Everyone's a ho in one way or another. So, baby, what up?"

"Been working."

Aja shook her head. "On New Year's Day? You work too hard. You need time to chill."

"Work now, chill later." I went to my front gate and she followed, uninvited. Soon we were in my microloft, and I sat while she went straight to my refrigerator.

"How come it's almost empty? Don't you go to Safeway?" she asked.

"I'm never here. I eat out."

"Shit." She pulled out some eggs, stiff bacon and ancient cheese. The she went through the rest of my minuscule excuse for a kitchen and found other presumably edible items and added them to the eggs and whatnot. I sat back and sighed, uninterested in the verbal give-and-take with Aja that she had always enjoyed.

"How come this place stinks?" she asked.

"'Cause *I* stink and I live here."

She started chopping ingredients together, with much speed and expertise. Aja could do many things very well, and I'd always resented her for that.

"I'm gonna give you one good meal today," she said, dumping the pile of chopped-up stuff into the skillet and turning on the heat. "One of the things about dope? It makes you hungry and makes every meal the best thing you've ever had. When I was famished and food just wasn't available, I'd just smoke some weed and the hunger pangs would disappear."

"For real? You've stopped getting high?"

"Yeah, baby. No crack, smack or even weed." Then, "Once I made the decision to stop using, I started going to meetings, and that helped for a while. But then they said, 'Surrender to a higher power.'" She turned to look at me. "Well, baby, there ain't no higher power than Captain Jack, and if you think there is, one of us is a fool."

I started to nod off. Aja sang and hummed, which soothed me, and the smell of delicious cooking filled my nostrils. A tasty meal always turned me on, especially when someone else had cooked it. I felt a tap on my shoulder and opened my eyes.

"Dig in," Aja said as I reached out and accepted a steaming omelet. She pulled up another chair and sat facing me. We both devoured our food. She asked, "Who lives in this building, anyway?"

"I dunno. People who can't afford anything better, I guess."

"The Tenderloin sucks. Always has, always will."

I shook my head. "It's being gentrified."

"It'll still be the Tenderloin."

I took a close look at her under the harsh light and could see lines and crow's feet. Aja had lived fast, loved hard and aged poorly. Her gauntness was becoming more pronounced. She swallowed a mouthful of food and said, "It's weird to me that you're a private detective. Of course, it was weird that you were a cop."

"Well, I had to do something. Besides, being a private eye is sometimes better than being a cop. I'm my own boss. I get to do the investigations my way. Don't have to wear blue, have a badge and be called a nigger or a pig a dozen times per day."

"You're dealing with a homicide case right now, aren't you? Sounds like cop work to me."

"It started out as a routine arson investigation. By the way, you know the people involved."

"Really?" she asked. "Who?"

"The Normans. Air conditioners. Remember Brynne Norman?"

"Well, her sister Ophelia was killed by the bomb."

Aja frowned and stopped eating. "That Missus Terryman was Brynne's sister? Damn. Nobody ever tells me anything."

I told her much of what I knew about the case. If I had been retained by a client, I wouldn't have said anything to Aja about my investigation. But since I was doing this on my own time, I decided to talk. Aja was a good listener; she paid attention and asked pertinent questions. It felt good to talk to someone, and our dinnertime conversation reminded me of when we were a couple. We went on forever back then about whatever was on our minds.

We finished dinner. My mind and body reminded

me that I was unwell. I shivered and yawned, then pulled down my bed, grabbed my quilt and covered myself as I sat facing Aja. "Why did you dump me, Aja? You went and left me all alone."

She thought for a moment. Her dimples appeared. I knew her answer would be less than I wanted.

"It wasn't you, sweetie. There was shit goin' on that I needed to work through. It was no personal rejection of you."

"You mean there was nobody else?"

Her dimples reappeared. She toyed with her fork and stared at her plate as if, written on it, were the words she wanted to say to me. She stretched her legs and stared at nothing for a few moments. "I wish I could make you understand, Coolidge. There was no one else, yet there were a zillion others. I guess I wanted more from life than you could give."

"What did you want," I asked her, "that I couldn't provide?"

She shrugged. "I wanted to be free, to do my thing and go my way and experience as much as I could. I didn't want to be anyone's woman, and you definitely had the attitude, 'Aja, you are my woman. I own you.' You smothered me."

"You seemed to lack a conscience."

She nodded. "Guilty as charged. I was no conscience and you were all conscience. That kept coming up. You kept getting freaked out by my behavior and I was, like, 'For fuck's sake, Cool, lighten up and chill out.'"

I shook my head. "I am not 'all conscience.' I am a liar. It's part of my job. I bullshit people all day and sleep like a baby all night."

She smiled. "Yeah. You were a liar. So was I. I

knew we had *something* in common." She looked at me
and I at her. I was startled by her eyes; how old and
tired they appeared. I could remember being with her,
gazing into her face and wondering if such a beautiful
woman had ever existed or would ever again. For
some reason, I have always expected the people I find
attractive to be empty vessels. I had seen Aja on stage
before I heard her sing, and assumed right away that
she was another no-talent bimbo who had gotten by
on her looks. Then I heard her belt out an old Aretha
song and nearly wept with longing. She strapped on a
guitar and played it as if it were merely an extension
of herself. I met, dated and married her, but we had
nowhere to go but down and apart. She lived for her
music, freedom, drugs and me, in that order. She had
too many things to live for, so she had to give up
something. Goodbye, Coolidge.

I sat there and stirred. Her forehead gleamed with
perspiration and I inhaled her scent, a hot dusky
aroma that I recognized at once and could not
imagine ever forgetting. I have observed that, in being
sexual with women, the normal rules do not apply
when getting it on with a former lover. Aja had
trained me well—or maybe she had simply ruined me
for all other women. Even after so many years, she
could, without effort, do things to me: Turn me on,
drive me crazy. I closed my eyes and looked away, as
if to avoid a hypnotist's spell. "You're seeing a
therapist. What's that all about?"

"He's a shrink. He's trying to help me get my shit
together."

"Did he send you over here to do some
'unfinished business' with me as part of your
treatment?"

"Part of it, yes. He thinks you and I should reconnect. It's a bad idea, but he's, like, the world's greatest expert on practically everything."

"Is he in love with you? Does he want to fuck you?"

She laughed. "He's gay. He's, like, 'Aja, you're broken but I want to fix you.' He doesn't think *he's* broken just because he's queer."

"Maybe *you* could straighten *him* out," I said. She laughed, all dimples and teeth and husky noise. But I sensed something unhappy in her laughter, and she sighed, slapping her thigh.

"Well, I gotta git," Aja said, picking up the plates and putting them into the sink. By seven, she had gone downstairs to get her jalopy. I cringed at the sound of its ancient engine as she pulled away from the curb.

My apartment now seemed darker and more desolate, as if robbed of something precious and life-giving. I locked my door and took a shower, hoping it would somehow make me feel better. Then I pulled down my bed, wrapped myself in my quilt and stared out into the darkness. Seeing Aja again made me feel the tiniest prick of an old familiar pain, one for which there was no cure and that I had hoped never to experience again.

Being in love with, and married to, a druggie is a great thing if you're turned on by loneliness and agony. Her constant faithlessness will keep you up nights, your mind racing. Some women roam and wander, trying to keep the party going or looking for the next one. They simply don't come home, and you lay in bed, thinking, *What if she's wrecked the car again? Maybe she's drunk and in jail? Or someone's robbed her, or*

171

she's overdosed? But what totally freaks you out is, *Maybe she's met someone she likes better than me.* The night seems an eternity, and each time you hear a car, you think it's her. But dawn arrives, even though you wish it wouldn't, and you can't decide if you want her to come home or drop dead.

Aja Harvey taught me to value aloneness. What I endure now is negligible compared to what I put up with when we were together.

19

The Normans held a memorial service for Ophelia on Sunday at two in the afternoon at the Universalist Church. They did it fast and simple, and limited the occasion to family and close friends. I sat, all dressed in black, in the back row, and some of the people who noticed me pointed me out to others. Maybe they didn't know that Ophelia knew a black person. I saw hella flowers but no casket; I guessed there hadn't enough left of the decedent to put into one. Only the preacher spoke—he invited them to do so, but no family member got up and eulogized their dead girl—and he said nothing about God or how she had gone on to a better place. Edina, Lloyd and Brynne sat there, dry-eyed. Allison and her mother cried passionately, their shoulders heaving. Cody sat alone in the front row, his face buried in his hands.

After the service, we convened to the small garden in the back to console each other over white wine and yummy dainty sandwiches. The conversation was polite but quiet and strained; I thought it wouldn't hurt them to lighten up, maybe even laugh. The sky was clear, the sun big and hot; I observed no sign of the fog or breeze, so common to this area, that would have made us all far more comfortable.

I went over and sat next to Allison on the bench next to the chapel door. She looked full of despair; I bet she hadn't eaten or slept well lately, and her hair was showing some gray. Her dark dress showed too much skin; her chest was freckled and lined. Soon she would be a frowzy, dumpy matron, and she was probably OK with that. Being young was just not her thing. We sat there together like little kids, our thighs pressed together. I was mostly unknown to these people, who were maybe thinking, *Who is that big black man and why is he getting so chummy with Allison Norman?*

"Where is Edina? I can't see her here," I said.

"She left as soon as the service was done." Allison sighed. "She's so cold and detached. Nothing ever gets to her."

"Brynne said Edina really lost it when she first heard about Ophelia and that bomb. Now she's got her self-control back, and I guess that's a good thing. Were Edina and Ophelia tight?"

Allison shrugged. "I'd always thought so."

"Look, Allison," I said, "people cope with these awful things in their own ways. I went to a funeral once where the dead person was a young guy who loved to tell jokes. The dead guy was young and had been killed in an auto accident. Some of his friends got up and told the guy's favorite jokes, and the dead guy's mom, who had heard all the jokes many times, well, she laughed so hard she pissed her pants. Her only child had just died, and she laughed because she was in shock. A few weeks later, she was hospitalized for major depression, anxiety and insomnia."

"Hmm." Then, "Did you know that Cody got another call from that crazy lady?"

"Brandy Capwell?"

"Yeah, whoever threatened to kill him."

"Did he call the cops?"

"Probably not. The crazy lady called him just before he left to come here."

Just then I saw Cody talking to some woman, and he saw me. I said, "Allison, I need to talk to Cody. I'll be back as soon as I can."

Cody left the woman and met me in a corner of the garden. He looked as burned and harrowed as I did. We had that in common, if nothing else.

Before he could say anything, I asked, "Did Brandy Capwell call you this morning?"

He nodded. "She's in San Francisco," he muttered. "She wants to see me."

"Don't do it."

"But she says she has information that could really be of use to me."

"She tried to kill you a few days ago. She killed your wife. Get the cops after her."

"I asked her about that, and she assured me she

175

had no part in any of it."

"Oh? And you believed her?"

He shrugged. "She sounded sincere."

"Well, if you won't call the cops, I will. Did she tell you her local address?"

"No. She wants to meet with me at the zoo. She said, 'Bring Cool Jones with you. He flew out to Chicago and we had a meeting.' Did you really? You didn't tell me that."

"I suppose I should have. I flew out there because I needed to figure out what happened to Huey Capwell, to see if his murder and the warehouse fire are related."

"Are they?"

"Maybe. Probably. I just don't know how yet."

"Huey's death was ruled a suicide," Cody said. "What makes you say murder?"

"Brandy Capwell says so."

"And if the crazy lady says so, it must be true."

"Well, it seems very suspicious that the lab work on Huey's dead body should just disappear the way it did. That makes me Brandy may be right. And the bomb that went off? Maybe that was the same person who had a different motive."

"I doubt that Huey died of anything other than carbon-monoxide poisoning," Cody said. "And if it was murder, I doubt the killer would say, 'I used carbon monoxide last time, so I think I'll use a bomb this time.'"

I shrugged and said, "I don't know what to tell you, Cody. But we're dealing with some serious stuff here. Time to call in the cops."

Cody looked away, so I looked where he was looking, and we watched Brynne approach us. She looked old and dried up. All of the Normans had been weakened by Ophelia's death, but Brynne looked much older now—tired, puffy eyes, grim mouth. She had a girlish face that didn't express profound emotion; now that Ophelia had been taken from her, she looked pouty and resentful, as if robbed of a favorite toy. "I'm taking Mom home," she told Cody.

He nodded. "OK, I'll be right with you." To me, he said, "Do you want to call Lando or shall I?"

"Let me. If there's anything worth reporting, I'll tell you about it. I'll meet you at the zoo at six."

I was back home just after three, but had some difficulty contacting Lando, who definitely wanted to speak to Brandy Capwell. He would show up at five in an unmarked car in case she got freaked out by the presence of the police. I changed into Levi's, a sweatshirt and sneakers. I didn't want to drive out to the zoo. I felt tired and bitchy, still needing to mend. My stamina wasn't nearly back to normal. About Brandy Capwell, I concurred with Cody. She seemed so unlikely to be bombing someone's house or have any culpability in her husband's death. She may have flipped out on the phone when she called Cody and said some nasty shit, but I couldn't see her offing anyone. I had met my share of killers, and she wasn't that kind of person. Of course, sometimes the nicest people turned out to be killers, so one could never be sure. Also, there remained the possibility that Brandy Capwell was simply who she said she was—someone with potentially valuable information.

I parked in the lot just outside the zoo's entrance and climbed out of my car. I hadn't been here in years and thought for a moment about the Christmas a few years ago when a few kids started taunting one of the tigers, who got pissed and leaped over the thirty-foot wall. The big cat killed one kid and injured another before the cops shot her dead. Poor kitty.

The sky turned the darkest gray and the wind blew hard. I loved these kinds of nights. I waved as Lando drove in and parked beside mine. We said hidy and made the smallest of talk until Cody pulled in, too. The three of us waited, and waited, and waited for Brandy Capwell. At just past eight, we said fuck it. Cody took Lando's number and said, "If I hear from her, you'll hear from me." We all felt disappointed by Brandy's failure to appear; we were eager to get the information she had more or less promised us. Cody seemed grateful to be around a couple of men who clearly wanted to help him and make his life easier by meeting the "crazy lady" with him. I supposed it would be very difficult for him to spend his first night alone as a brand-new widower. He'd spent the night at his mother-in-law's house while the bomb squad investigated what was left of his Lafayette home and a work crew boarded up what the bomb had blown away.

My own mood plummeted. I hated starting a new year with a funeral, especially when the thing that killed the other person almost got me, too. The Tylenol 3s I had been popping slowed me down and made me goofy and sluggish. I felt lonely and needed someone to love—someone who would love me back. I wanted to put on that ruined Versace suit and go out for an evening of bright lights and loud voices. I wanted a steak dinner with red wine, cheesecake for dessert and lots of silly talk. Then I wanted to dance till two in the morning. I liked to think of myself as

Mr. Tough Guy, the man who needed only himself, but it was easy to see how quickly people came to depend on each other.

I drove home admitting to myself that I hoped Aja would be there waiting for me. Aja was unpredictable in so many ways. She had left me, all those years earlier, without a word or note. She hated to deal with people's attitudes and dramas; why deal with their shit when she could just walk away? She said that people who were clingy and morose and suicidal freaked her out. Her thing was to step aside and say, "I'm not going to help you cope with your crisis, because that's no fun. Call me when you feel better." I had watched her do that to her own people, her friends and family; she'd quit promising musical gigs because they bored her, or because someone in charge insisted that she sing a song in a way she disliked. One day she would just plain disappear and not reappear for a couple of years. By then, you'd forgotten most or all of you conflict with her, and she would instantly win you over again with her deep dimples, big brown eyes and Hey Baby charisma.

With me, because I had been in love with Aja and married to her, some of my anger and hurt had remained following our breakup. Aja would literally scratch her head with incomprehension at my inability to forgive and forget her transgressions. I could not make my sociopathic wife understand that I thought it mean and bad for her to run off and fuck other men. Ragging on her seemed about as futile as trying to train a house cat to roll over or fetch my slippers. Moreover, the woman had more games than Toys R Us. She was liberated, manipulative, carefree, sensuous, romantic, spontaneous. Music, dancing, going places, hanging out, making love…she did such things better than anyone I had ever met. Until she lost interest in her companion, or got a better offer from someone else, and off she went. I had never been intimate with someone like Aja, so she taught me much about many things. The problem was, I really didn't want to learn such things.

Back home, I got the last space in the parking lot. Aja was back on Turk Street, leaning against her car. She had a shopping bag with her. I could see French bread sticking out.

"Thought you would be in Los Angeles by now," I told her.

"I'm feeling so welcome here," she retorted, "that I thought I might just stay on a while."

"I hope you're not going to sleep in your car," I said.

"This is the Tenderloin. There's always a cheap room available no matter the time of day or night."

"Just make sure you get a place with no bedbugs." Then, "Whatcha got there in that bag?"

"Food," she said. "I find that if I go a few days or more without eating, my health deteriorates."

"How long have you been parked out here?"

"An hour or two. Cool, are you sure you should be pulling these long hours? You look even worse than when I saw you earlier."

I sighed. "I feel worse than dead. Come on up. You got wine in there?"

She followed me as I opened the front gate and took the elevator up. When we reached my suite, she emptied her bag and we gorged ourselves on wine, bread, pate, cold cuts, salad and chocolate cake. As I sat back, more than sated, she began to sing a cappella: gospel songs, rhythm-and-blues classics and things I had never heard of. She didn't sing them so much as make love to them, exploring and embroidering melodies, lingering on this part and hurrying through that one.

Then she just stopped.

"Something the matter?" I asked.

She sat pouting, as if ready to cry. "I don't have it anymore. It all went away when I stopped using."

"Huh?"

"You heard me. I made the choice to give up the drugs. But it's no drugs, no music, and I can't live without the music."

"You still have it, Aja. Your voice is beautiful."

"You don't know jackshit about music, Coolidge. That was nothing. It was just vocal exercise. My soul is gone. The only way I can make my music come alive and be beautiful is when I'm high on blow. I need the dope to set me free and let my music happen. Otherwise it's just all stuck inside me and can't get out. You feel me?"

I frowned and tried to understand. "So you're saying...what? That you want to start taking drugs again because it'll help your music?"

Aja closed her eyes and said nothing, the way she had done during our marriage when reaching out to me only to discover that I wasn't there for her. Then she tapped on the crook of her arm, as if preparing to shoot up.

"Don't even think about it," I said. "If you do it, you'll never get clean again. You'll just kill yourself."

"Well, so what? 'Go for the gusto, right?"

"Wrong."

"'Reality is for people who can't handle drugs.'"

"Very clever."

"Life without drugs is boring as hell. How do you do it?"

"One day at a time, Aja. Eat, sleep, work. You get used to it. You get to like it. You get 'high on life.'"

She shook her head. "You're so lame."

I gathered up all of our disposal debris into the large shopping bag she'd brought. She sat on the floor, her head drooping, hands in her lap. I doubted she would live more than a few more years.

"Did you come back here to dump this shit all over me?" I asked her. "Do you want my permission to puke on heaven's door?"

"Yes, please."

I took the bagful of trash and put it into a huge plastic trash bag, which I then tied, to make it ready for the dumpster. I stared at Aja, thinking that she'd wasted her whole life preparing for, and eagerly awaiting, the one man she truly loved: the Grim Reaper.

"Go away and never come back, Aja," I said. "Do me that one favor, OK?"

20

I got up on Monday morning at six o'clock and jogged for five miles. I still felt pretty banged up and was a fool to push myself that hard, but this Christmas had sucked balls and the new year was pretty fucked up, too. We were a few days into January and my inner spoiled brat started throwing a temper tantrum, demanding that my life return to what it had been before the bullshit began. I hoped Orlanda would come back and reopen her tavern and that Roberta would return home, too. Emma was due back on Friday, and as I ran uphill, I reminded myself that I was the luckiest son of a bitch who'd ever lived, even if my body ached liked one big impacted tooth, Mutual had kicked me out of my office and someone had stuck that five grand into my checking account last month to make me look corrupt.

The sky was a light gray, the breeze gentle for the moment. If you're in San Francisco and you don't like the weather, just wait fifteen minutes; if you're here and don't like your neighbors, wait another fifteen. The city's natural coolness made my jogs easier; its natural hills did not. By the time I'd finished and returned to my front gate, my face, arms and legs were gleaming with sweat and my T-shirt was drenched. But the main thing was, I'd worked off much of my anxiety, and my endorphins once again made America beautiful. On Turk Street, Aja had moved her car; its replacement was a small car covered by a cheap-looking gray cover. Parking, even in the Tenderloin, was often difficult to find in the city, and I wondered if that cover protected a Bugatti or some other exotic machine that car thieves might consider worth their trouble.

Lloyd Norman called me at eight o'clock. The mediocre reception indicated to me that he was using his cell phone.

"You sound like you're calling from Mars," I told him.

"I'm in my car. Might as well be Mars. I'm pretty sure they've bugged my office phone."

"Have you had anyone check it out yet?"

"I don't know how to do it and I'm not going to have the phone company send out a technician to do it for me."

"Why are you under the impression your phone is bugged?"

"This and that. I'll make a confidential remark on the phone and soon everyone knows about it. I know that people have big mouths and repeat all kinds of shit, but I've been on the phone with out-of-state customers and people out here suddenly know what I said to the out-of-staters even though they had no way of knowing. This is making me look like quite a chump. Would you help me with it?"

"OK. First, unscrew the receiver on your bugged phone and look for the bug itself."

"I wouldn't know a phone bug if it started buzzing and tried to bite me," he said.

"Maybe the phone isn't bugged. Maybe the bug is somewhere else in the office."

"And what would I do about *that*?"

"There's a handheld scanner many electronics stores carry. I'm surprised I don't own one myself. I'll try to buy one before I drive out to the plant. I'll get there as soon as I can, but I have other things to do today."

"OK. Thanks." Click.

I spent the next hour reading and revising my notes on the Norman warehouse fire. I also dialed Brandy Capwell's Chicago number in case her roommate was in and had some information on how I might contact Brandy.

At just after nine, my phone rang. Mercedes, at the other end, spoke barely above a whisper. "Bad news, Cool."

I groaned.

"If I change the subject in mid-sentence, you'll know the big man has just walked in." She meant

185

Lowell. "He was talking to Jeri and said that someone told the cops about the warehouse inventory. Apparently Lloyd Norman moved all of the merchandise out of the warehouse and into another facility before the fire happened. The stuff he wanted to be reimbursed for? It was all just garbage."

"No way," I told her. "I went out there myself and did an investigation. I looked through half a dozen boxes. They lost some valuable stuff in that blaze."

"Maybe they left behind a few boxes of actual merchandise to make it look more believable," Mercedes said. "Lloyd is going to be charged with arson and fraud. You're being named as a conspirator. Lowell has turned the file over to the district attorney. I thought you should know this right away so you can see a lawyer."

"Any idea on how fast they're gonna move on this thing?"

"Mister Stanich isn't in today, but if you leave a message I'll be sure that he gets it."

Click.

I called Kenny Longman and ran it down for him. "I don't know about any charges," he said. "I'll call the D.A.'s office and ask if they've issued a warrant for your arrest."

"What should I do now?" I asked.

"Wait for my call. If they've issued the warrant, turn yourself in. You will spare yourself the humiliation of leaving your apartment in police custody."

"Shit, this is a nightmare."

"Nothing has happened yet. If the nightmare starts, don't panic. Your lawyer will help. If you're innocent, you have nothing to worry about."

"Famous last words."

After hanging up, I walked over to Market Street and found a store that carried electronics-surveillance scanners. The device I bought, about the size of a Walkman, was adequate for the detection of most bugging frequencies. The selection of these gadgets overwhelmed me at first; not in years had I needed to deal with checking for, or planting, bugs in people's homes or offices. To plant it, one had to put on a phony uniform, enter the premises and put the bug in there so that no one would ever discover it. That kind of activity I expensive, illegal in many states and a hell of a lot more challenging than what we see in Hollywood spy movies. Today, folks don't fuck around with that bugging shit—they just shot each other. Bang, bang, end of beef. There was always the chance that Lloyd Norman was just getting paranoid, but I had a feeling he had a legitimate cause for concern.

All during my drive to Oakland, I kept my windows down and enjoyed the feel of the wind whipping my face. I liked living surrounded by water on three sides. Kept Cool cool. Let the people in the East Bay cope with those sweltering summers.

I parked right in front of Norman Appliances and Lloyd stood there waiting for me, his shirt wrinkled and sleeves rolled up.

"Do we have to stay silent because of the bug?" he asked as we entered his office.

"No, just be yourself. If they know we know about the bug, good for us."

Lloyd sighed. "If there's a bug, we'll never find it."

"If there's a bug, and it was planted by the FBI or

CIA, we'd never find it because they're experts at bugging. They could have put the damn thing anywhere, including the exterior of the building or the telephone line. But I'm pretty sure we're dealing with amateurs, so the thing is probably right here and it'll be easy enough to find."

He pointed at his computer. "Maybe they've put a little man in there. He can see us but we can't see him. He's watching us and telling the bad guys what we're up to."

"Then I'll just smash the machine and if the little man is in there, I'll give him a Cool Jones beatdown."

He pointed at my new toy and asked, "What's that?"

"Bug detector. If there's a bug, this detector will hear it squeal. If that doesn't work, we'll check out the rest of the office." I switched on the gadget and started waving it with the greatest care across the room, then on the floor, like one of those weird old guys at the beach with a metal detector, searching for loot.

Zilch.

Little man, where *are* you?

Just then, I noticed the telephone jack by the office door. "Phone jack but no phone," I said to Lloyd.

He shrugged. "Had the phone connected to the other jack last time I had my furniture moved."

I lay down on the floor and peered at the jack. It looked normal enough. It got out my Army knife and unscrewed the switchplate. I put my hand into the hole and pulled out a voice recorder not much bigger than a credit card that had been cut in half.

"Hello, little man." A little red light indicated that

the recorder was on. I turned it off.

Lloyd let out a huge sigh. "I was right. Unfortunately."

"Any idea who your enemies might be?"

He threw out his arms. "Didn't know I had any."

"It appears that you do. Someone wasted Huey Capwell and would have gotten Cody Terryman except that Ophelia got to the bomb first. What do you three boys have in common?"

"Just this company. So, if someone wanted to take over Norman Appliances, why would they kill the people who run it?"

"Maybe it's something that has nothing to do with the company. People kill each other for all kinds of reasons. They could be after your money."

"They're after something." He wiped sweat off his brow and pushed the bug towards me. "I appreciate your help."

"There may be more of these. That one was easy to find. The next one may be harder."

I picked up my knapsack and walked towards the door. "Lloyd, make sure you call or email me if you hear anything I should know. If Brandy Capwell contacts you, tell me about it as soon as you can."

I looked to my left and saw Sal Johnson, the chemical engineer, perusing some material. "Yes?"

"Is Davida Avalon here?" I asked.

"She's stepped out for a moment. She'll be back in a few minutes."

I handed him my business card. "Have her call me."

He nodded.

By three o'clock I had returned to my microloft, exhausted from that trip to Oakland but pleased that I had accomplished something. I dropped my knapsack on the floor and, inside it, the bug detector shrieked like a woman whose ass had just been grabbed. I snatched the device out of my bag and turned it off. Feeling parched and hot, I opened my refrigerator, praying for a can of Bud that I knew wasn't there. I didn't even have any sodas left. Shitfuck!

I stood there and thought for the longest time. Had they done me like they did Lloyd? I turned the detector back on and it screamed like a siren. I stepped over to the corner where Aja's harmonica remained in its case. Next to the brass lock, a quarter-sized bug had been taped to the case. I felt out of breath, as if someone had just punched me in the solar plexus. Aja, too, seemed out to get me.

21

So, I asked myself, who asked Aja to bug my place? I guessed Edina or Brandy Capwell. One or the other had approached her. No-conscience Aja didn't care if she fucked me over—she'd had years of experience at it. I shuddered at the thought of how much information about me Aja had acquired, and how many insights she had gained into my life and work. Her bug had enabled her to record my phone conversations. Maybe that was how Vince Stanich had learned that Mercedes and I were after him. Ophelia's death had appeared in the online news services the day *after* his disappearance. Had Vince known about the bomb? I needed to find Aja and ask her about these things.

I collected her harmonica case and surveillance device and stowed her shit in the trunk of my car. Then I got in and cruised around the Tenderloin, looking for that sorry excuse for a car she had been driving. I went up and down Eddy, Ellis, Turk, O'Farrell and Golden Gate. No Aja. After I gave up, I drove back home. When I got to my front gate, I noticed the car with the cover. Worse, I smelled something vile, even worse than the urine and feces one can always smell in my 'hood. The smell had to be coming from that car under the cover. As a cop, I had caught a whiff of things so horrid I could never entirely forget their stench, and those disgusting, rotten things were always covered up with something. Although I wanted just to go back up to my suite and let the covered car become someone else's problem, I walked up to the car, my eyes tearing and nose running, and pulled up a section of the gray cover, already knowing what was there, stinking so much.

Still, I tore my hand away, as if from a white-hot door handle, and emitted the kind of guttural groan that grown men usually don't make.

Brandy Capwell sat leaning against the passenger's side window, her eyes freakishly huge but totally sightless, her face blown up to nearly twice its normal size, tongue blackened and swollen, protruding from purple lips. I found something grotesquely mirthful in her expression, as if she had died making a playful face and trying to stick out her tongue at her strangler.

I took out my iPhone and called 911 to report my

discovery. I sounded matter-of-fact; I felt detached and indifferent, the way I had done when, as a cop, I dealt with dreadful and disturbing things. I remembered meeting with her in that O'Hare bar, liking her even though I had expected not to, feeling sorry that she'd had widowhood thrust upon her so suddenly and prematurely. Convinced that her late husband had been murdered, she persuaded me that she was right. Now she had joined him in death.

The dispatcher assured me that a car was on the way, which of course there was, because this was the Tenderloin. I stood there, next to the covered car with the hideous odor, and breathed through my mouth. Passersby pinched their noses and shot me dirty looks.

The cruiser rounded the corner as I stood by the death car, waving as if hailing a taxi. The two cops inside, Geary and Lankford, were people I had known for a while and who had seen grislier things than a bloated corpse. In my time, I had seen corpses, one or two jumpers who did the deed while we were trying to talk them down. My most memorable was with one lonely fellow who went into a porno shop to beat off and smoke crack in one of the private booths. Trouble was, he accidentally set himself on fire and ran screaming out of the store. I was on duty when I saw the human inferno, and literally tripped him so he would fall and I could try to pat down some of his flames with my gloved hands. Within moments, the firefighters arrived, put him out and shipped him off to Memorial's burn unit. I heard he had third-degree burns over ninety percent of his body. They probably put him into a coma and let him die.

Here on Turk Street, I believed that the killing of Brandy and the positioning of her body—face pressed up against the window of the car, staring at my front gate—was a message intended for me personally, though I did not understand its meaning. I empathized with the Normans over the death of Ophelia but did not believe that I had been targeted that evening. It was just my bad luck that I had been so physically close to her when the package detonated. The covered car containing Brandy's corpse freaked me out. I felt surprised and relieved that the killer hadn't left a note on the window saying YOU'RE NEXT, MOTHERFUCKER. Some bastard out there had gone to hella trouble to put that car there with her rotting body inside it.

For the next while, the police owned that part of Turk Street. Officers, cars, the coroner's wagon, and Coolidge Jones. Although now a civilian, I had been one of them not so very long ago and knew the drill as well as they did, so they got what they needed from me nice and fast. The problem of Brandy Capwell and who might be the next victim was now theirs as much as mine.

The car turned out to be a rental—Avis this time, not Rent a Piece of Shit. I had seen the vehicle for the first time that morning, and I remembered thinking it odd that a car valuable enough to deserve a cover should be parked on Turk Street. While I knew the decedent from flying out to O'Hare for a few glasses of wine and some talk, I didn't know when she had gotten in, although of course I knew that she claimed to have valuable information for Cody Terryman. Lando had gone to the zoo with me so he knew all about her failure to appear. She was probably dead by then and her body had begun to decay.

I did not want to look at the death car again but did so anyway. The medical examiner was busy with his preliminary examination of the deceased. He had opened all of the car's doors and released Brandy's reek out into the street, the way an oil refinery's putrid gases foul an entire valley. By then the sky had turned the darkest gray and working people in business attire who were passing through stepped to the other side of the street and waved their hands in front of their faces, even as they gawked at the crime scene with the same morbid fascination as rubberneckers checking out a mangled car or two in a wreck where blood had been spilled onto the roadway. The gawkers pointed at the bright lights that had been set up so that the crime technicians could dust the entire vehicle for fingerprints.

Geary had borrowed my iPhone to call Avis and tell them about their car. As soon as he finished, he handed me back my iPhone and I watched as the coroner's boys zipped Brandy Capwell into a plastic bag. She had bloated so much that, even though I knew better, I felt afraid she would, like a pricked balloon, burst right there in front of me.

I hurried back up to my apartment and, after stripping down to my birthday suit, stuffed all of my clothing into a plastic bag and took a shower. As the hot water ran down my face and body, I flashed on the vastness of O'Hare Airport and my folksy, good-humored companion that evening, who seemed to find some good in life despite losing her husband and being reduced to mixing drinks in an airport bar. Although I hated pitying people, particularly myself, I pitied her, and maybe both of us. She had loved Huey and lost him to death; I had loved Aja but lost her, perhaps because she had no love, for me or anyone else, and probably considered me unworthy of loving her, anyway.

By nine o'clock, the police and coroner had left and the Tenderloin had returned to normal, so to speak. I felt too agitated to stay in my microloft, so I got dressed, grabbed my knapsack, climbed into my car and started cruising the neighborhood, looking for Aja's car.

I smiled as I pulled into the parking lot of the Hotel Phoenix, a place legendary among musicians. Aja's jalopy sat parked in front of room number three, and next to it was a BMW convertible. After getting out and locking my car, I went over to the Beemer, opened its glove box and withdrew the pink slip. Registered owner was Lloyd Norman. Hmm.

I knocked on Aja's door, seeing that the lights were on. Still, she took forever to open the door, and when she did so, she peered out at me through a crack. She seemed muzzy and embarrassed, if still half-asleep and standing there in her undies or birthday suit.

"Hey," I murmured. "Ain't y'all gonna invite me in?"

She sighed and stepped aside so I could enter. She stood there naked but for a black thong, and she crossed her arms over her breasts. I smirked at the sight of the closed bathroom door. I made a loud sniffing noise at the musky, funky odor that filled the room. Fucking is a smelly business.

"I brought your Bob Dylan harmonica. It's in the trunk of my car."

"You didn't have to do that. I was going to come

by and get it," she said.

"Hey, I wanted to see you and talk to you. We used to be married, right?" I made a point of looking around the room. I could smell weed along with the scent of sweat and hormones. I spotted a packet or two of condoms, a crumpled latex glove, a flesh-colored dildo. I pointed at her paraphernalia. "Got some company, huh? Gettin' friendly, too. At least you're bein' responsible and practicin' safe sex."

She stared at me for a few moments. She had known me long enough to tell that I was in a supremely foul mood. "Is there something I can do for you? I'm kinda busy."

"Yeah, you're kinda busy." White people had never been Aja's thing, so far as I knew—mine, neither—but then, with Aja, who the fuck knew? "I found the bug in your harmonica case. Do you want it back? Surveillance equipment isn't cheap, you know. Thank you, Aja, for coming back into my life and doing me like that again."

Aja just looked at me. She didn't deny anything. I strode over and threw open the bathroom door.

Brynne, sitting on the toilet, smiled at me, her face the deepest red. A stinging pain began in my chest and traveled through down to my toes, and then I lost all feeling. I did not even feel rage, disgust or humiliation when I realized that Aja and Brynne were lovers. When had I last seen them together? At Brynne's birthday party, held at a local country club. Aja had sung there and I had attended the event as a guest because of my friendship with Allison. Aja. A couple of weeks later, Aja departed without saying goodbye, at about the same time that Brynne, too, had fucked off in her own search of musical fame.

Now I knew why Aja had taken off like she did. Which of the two had made the first move? How long had they been together? Did it matter? Was it any of my business?

Brynne threw a towel around herself, and I had a look at the woman my ex had taken as her lover. Tall, skinny women like her really didn't do it for me, but I admired her comportment, the way I had always thought highly of Brynne because she had read books, traveled widely and carried herself in that way rich people had because rich people had the time and means to work on walking, talking and looking proper, while all the rest of us were just working to get a paycheck and feed our families.

"Good evening, Coolidge," Brynne murmured as she ducked past me and entered the bedroom. Stopping at the nightstand, she plucked the half-smoked joint out of the ashtray, lit it and took a couple of long, slow hits. She pointed at it and looked at Aja, who shook her head. The two women beamed at each other with such sisterly affection that I wondered if my entire life with Aja had been a lie.

Brynne looked over at me and asked, "So...Coolidge...to what do we owe the pleasure?"

"Brandy Capwell is dead."

"I'm sorry for your loss. Was she a friend of yours?"

"Her late husband worked for your family's company," I said. "I'm sure you remember Huey Capwell."

She took another hit and put the joint back in the ashtray, then lay back on the bed. "You don't have to be rude. I really don't have anything to do with the company except that I like to spend its money. Huey and Brandy and all the rest of it? That's *your* problem, not mine."

"Bullshit! The only reason I'm involved in this mess at all is that I used to work for Mutual of Northern California."

"My mother told me that the D.A.'s office is going to charge you with insurance fraud."

"And you think I'm guilty?"

"Well, maybe. Lloyd got into some financial trouble, so he torched his warehouse instead of getting a bank loan. To get the insurance money, he just needed a little help from his friends. Like you."

I chuckled. "For someone who's been out of town, you sure seem to know what's going on. Who gives you your information?"

"I know people."

"Maybe the information they've been giving you is bad."

"If it is bad, I'm sure you'll find the good information and see to it that the bad guys get busted. Isn't that what you're all about, Coolidge?"

I said to Aja, "What's eating you? Or is that an inappropriate way of putting it?"

Aja frowned and said nothing.

"We had to learn as much as we could," said Brynne, "and you weren't exactly forthcoming about this matter, Coolidge, so we had to do things to know what you knew. We're going to take what we have about your involvement and turn it over to the district attorney."

"What do you mean by 'we'?"

Brynne shrugged. "Just what I said."

"And Vince Stanich? What about him?"

"You tell me."

"Well, gee, Brynne, I don't have many details on Stanich, either. I had the impression that someone had scared him with threats so he took off. I figure he's out of town or dead, maybe both." Then, "Doesn't it upset you that Brandy Capwell was murdered?"

"Every death is a tragedy," Brynne said. "But I didn't know her, so my mourning will last about fifteen minutes. Anyway, I think she's gone off to a better place."

"There seems to be a killer on the loose who's already killed your sister. How can you be sure that you're safe and the killer is going to leave you alone?"

"Why are you under the impression," Aja asked, "that she knows who the killer is?"

"Because my impressions are usually right," I said.

22

When I got home, I felt worse than dead and too tired to sleep. I made sure my Glock was loaded and ready for action. I didn't like it that my window looked out onto Turk Street, and that anyone who wanted to toss a Molotov cocktail into my microloft could probably do so without much hassle. I also dreaded falling asleep and having nightmares starring Brandy Capwell.

So I pulled down my bed, crawled into it and let insomnia have its way with me. I turned on my TV and flipped through my scores of channels scores of times. I watched CNN mostly, and the early hours crept by as I stared at the TV screen and paid little or no attention as the overnight anchor tried to update me on the state of the world. I heard the occasional car go by, honking its horn, but mostly the street stayed quiet, and as I lay in my lonely little joke of an apartment, I pictured Aja, nearly a dozen blocks away, sleeping naked in Brynne's arms, my ex's breasts gathered together, nipples an inch apart.

I nodded off as night yielded to a soiled shade of gray. I woke up at just after eight, my TV still on, and I felt heavy headed and disoriented, knowing that I had many things to do that day and by noon would be as inert and insensible as a zombie. I wanted to meet up with Davida Avalon in Oakland as soon as Norman Appliances' business office opened, and that meant I would have to delay my morning run. I would need to cope for the rest of the day with the anxiety coursing through my brain and body, a malaise usually treatable by a long hard jog up and down my city's hills. Who needed to mainline smack when an endorphin high was legal and free?

I showered, shaved, dressed and made a pot of coffee that I poured into my Thermos. I drank it as I drove out to Oakland.

They expected Lloyd to be in at about ten, and Cody would be away till he felt well enough to return to work. Davida, however, sat at her desk, sneering at the work in front of her, if that's what it was.

"I left my business card with Sal," I told her as I sat down across from her. "I wanted you to call me."

"We're so busy, I just didn't have time." Davida looked at me with pursed lips. She cleared her throat.

"I heard the awful news about Brandy Capwell. I really don't what to think or say about it. It just breaks my heart."

"Did you know her?"

"No, we'd just talked on the phone once or twice. But her husband had worked here, and I was once married to a man who committed suicide, so I can't help but feel badly about Brandy."

"In her case, the husband's death wasn't absolutely verified as a suicide. She swore till the end that he'd been murdered. All of his remains disappeared before they could definitely determine the manner of death."

"On the radio, they really didn't say much about Brandy's death. I guess the reporters get their information from the police, and the police often don't tell very much. Do *you* know what happened?"

I nodded and told her most of what I knew. Her face contorted in revulsion, as if I had magically produced Brandy's putrid corpse and flopped it down onto Davida's desktop. Normally I don't like to gross people out that way, but in her case she really seemed interested and might repay the favor by telling me something I didn't already know.

"Mind if I smoke?" she asked. "I'm not supposed to—"

"We won't tell anyone."

She lit up a Newport and took a nice long hit. Then she closed her eyes and exhaled. "Yummy."

"Let's talk about Huey Capwell."

"I barely knew him. He did his job and I did mine. I hadn't been here that long when he died."

"Who was the office manager before you?"

"Nobody. It was total chaos here. Took me months to get everything straight and organized."

"How was morale here? Did people get along?"

Davida nodded. "Guy ran the place. He got along with everyone. Our product was the most popular one around. Great job security—no one worried about getting laid off, and everyone made better than decent money. No feuds that I knew of." Then, "Guy was bidding on a big government contract. The Army wanted a huge number of air conditioners for its bases, I think. We were getting ready to fill a big order if we won the contract."

"And…?"

She shrugged. "I guess we didn't get the order. I don't know what happened. Guy dropped dead around that time and Lloyd, for whatever reason, didn't pursue the contract." Davida saw Sal Johnson walk by. She said, "Sal, would you come here for a moment?"

He did so, and frowned with recognition as he saw me. "What's this about Brandy Capwell? My wife heard some awful story on the news."

I ran it down for him. "I'm trying to figure out how the Brandy Capwell murder ties in with Lloyd and the warehouse fire. I'm sure it all fits together."

"Lloyd isn't going to be charged with insurance fraud over our warehouse fire, is he?"

I nodded. "Him and me."

He shook his head. "Awful. I'm not sure what her murder and that government contract had in common, but I'll tell you what happened. One of Huey's jobs was to go online and find government contracts that might be a nice fit for us. He found one item, a request for bids to sell Uncle Sam an air conditioner that could cool the chemicals used to make nuclear bombs. Potentially dangerous work, and

Norman doesn't *make* those kinds of appliances, but we could do it if we got the contract, and then there would be the very tasty prospect of repeat business. It would have been a major challenge for us, and some of us thought it was too much trouble, but Guy was the boss and we needed to trust his judgment. He had a good feeling about this."

"How much money could Norman have stood to make on that deal?"

"Oh, hundreds of thousands. Probably millions if Uncle Sam liked our products and bought lots more."

"How close were you to winning the contract when Huey died?"

"Oh, I guess we were confident we'd get it. Huey had gone down to Los Angeles to get some documentation we needed from the Defense Department building there. Since it was a military contract, we needed clearances. I don't really think Huey's death made that much of a difference with that contract. But when Guy died, it really broke our hearts. We lost interest in that contract. We just kept doing what we had always done—build and sell our usual products to our customers."

"Could the company have handled that big government order even with Guy and Huey dead?"

He shrugged. "Oh, sure. Building the appliance that the government wanted would have been a challenge for us, but we could have done it. We missed out on a big opportunity, but it didn't cost us a dime. Around that time, Guy had just died and Lloyd was taking over. He didn't have any idea of how to run the company, so I don't think he was too eager to win a big government contract and cope with all that stress. So we didn't get that contract, and

Lloyd just sort of stood back and watched as the company ran itself."

"What about government contracts since then?"

"Not our thing. We don't go looking for them and they don't come looking for us."

I sighed and said, "Well, thanks for your time. I'll get back to you if I need to ask you some more questions."

"Glad to help." He got up and left.

Davida and I spoke for a little while longer and she told me nothing of significance except for one thing: Edina had attended Huey Capwell's memorial service.

"I thought she had moved to Europe and was married to some dumbass who couldn't decide what he wanted to be when he grew up."

"Yes, but she came back for a visit twice a year or so," Davida said.

"How long had she been back in town?"

"Oh, I have no idea. I don't know how they do things in that family, and they probably wouldn't tell me if I asked. I'm not one of theirs."

"Maybe I can find that out," I said.

On the drive back into San Francisco, I could have slapped myself upside the head. I had been wrong to assume that Edina and Brynne had alibis in the Huey Capwell death—they had been thousands of miles away. Now I knew that I needed to ask more questions, so I pulled over, took out my iPhone and called the Norman residence. Didn't matter which of them I spoke to. But when the maid answered, she said that Missus Norman was napping and therefore unavailable. Edina and Allison had gone out to buy themselves something nice to wear; Brynne would be back very soon. Did I wish to have one of them return my call?

I said no and hung up without telling her who I was. Then I called Stacey at Mutual, who told me she had nada to report but would leave a message on my machine if she learned anything I should know. Yeah, I thought, you do that.

I put my iPhone aside and drank the rest of my coffee. Caffeine and I got along real good. I knew I was getting close to solving this case, that I just needed to get straight answers to a few more questions and then I would say to Lando, "Here's the bad guy—lock his ass up."

I started up my car again and headed back towards the Bay Bridge, thinking, *Maybe Vince's girlfriend has something for me.* Not long afterwards, I stood at her building's front entrance just as someone left. I grabbed the gate before it closed and headed for Renee's suite, just as I had done on my earlier visit. Damn you, Cool, you've got to learn some manners.

I knocked on her door. I didn't know if she worked, didn't know what she did, where she went or what she was all about. I didn't want to get to know her any better than I had to. I heard her footsteps and watched her door swing open. I saw her glower as she eyeballed my pretty dark-brown face.

"Hello, I'm Coolidge Jones," I said, as bright and sincere as a Mormon elder out to snatch her soul away. "I'm still hoping to connect with Vince Stanich and I'm wondering if you've heard from him."

She kept glowering as she shook her head.

"He hasn't called you just to tell you he was OK?"

Another shake of the head.

"For real? I thought he would do that."

"No."

We shared a few moments of quiet in which I stared at her and she at me. She began to close the door the tiniest bit.

"How did Vince get that Norman account, anyway?" I wanted to know.

"Why ask me?"

"Did Vince know Lloyd? Or was it one of the other Normans?"

"Ask the Normans. Anyway, Vince was the claims manager. I don't think he sold policies—he just bossed people around."

"Really? I thought I saw on one of the forms that he was listed as the seller of the policy. Maybe that was his job before he was promoted to claims manager."

She blew out a big sigh. "You done yet?"

"Almost. Did Vince know any of the Normans?"

"You just asked me that."

"Your answer was unsatisfactory, so I'm going to keep asking till you give me what I want."

She glowered some more. "How the hell would I know who his friends are?"

"Well, I'm trying to figure out why he's been gone for several days and you don't seem to give a shit. What's up with that?"

"I'm sure he'll be in touch. Anything else?"

I nodded. "Maybe I'll go back to his place and see if there's something I missed."

"Have fun." She shut the door.

I walked back to my building, got into my car and drove out to Vince Stanich's big white building near the beach, mostly because I had nowhere else to go. I moved about in the dusty, neglected apartment with much interest. Vince lived with so few comforts that it looked as if he were just moving in or about to move out. As a private eye, I am always looking for clues, particularly receipts or messages that will tell me something. Vince's suite had plenty of paper scraps on the floor, so I got on my hands and knees to collect and read them. They revealed nothing to me, and I felt like a chump or being on all fours, reading someone's irrelevant shit.

23

I found a parking spot right across from Vince's building and felt relieved that I had no forms to fill out, no bitchy clients to rag on my ass. I did, however, know I had some big legal problems that were about to happen if I failed to figure out how all that money got into my checking account and who torched the Norman warehouse in Oakland. The bad guy responsible for all that shit had deliberately made it look like my doing. Someone had devised a scheme to make Lloyd look bad and eliminate two key people at Norman Appliances. Vince knew about all this and had participated in it, but as soon as Ophelia had been blown up into a thousand pieces all over Lafayette, he had hauled ass out of town. I needed to find out the link between Vince Stanich and the person who had gotten him to go along with this nasty scheme. Once I had that, I could put together all the pieces of the puzzle.

The Monterey's fire escape stood vacant and inviting, so I leapt up and grabbed hold of the lowest rung and pulled myself up. I hoped nobody had seen me do it, because they would almost certainly call the cops, I didn't expect to be in Vince's suite long enough to get caught there. I climbed like a cat and reached Vince's suite within a couple of minutes. I pulled up his window with no effort and let out a huge sigh. I would have considered kicking open the window if it had been locked, but that wasn't the case. I also felt a little anxious that I might find Vince's bloated, reeking body somewhere in there. But I found no dead fat guys, and the abundant dust made it clear that the place had been vacant for some time. I made a fast walkthrough, checking all the rooms and closing the drapes. Often, a private investigator will get his best information from scraps of paper on the floor, and Vince's suite had plenty of those, but they were all bullshit and I felt like a fool for getting on my hands and knees to check them out.

Vince had moved out, taking all the things that mattered most to him and leaving behind the things too big to fit into his car. His exercise equipment remained and so did his home office, such as it was: card table for a desk, a couple of lawn chairs and a telephone with an answering machine. This last item,

I believed, would give me the best clues as to Vince's most recent contact with the outside world. I poked around on his machine until I found the function for last numbers dialed. I punched the button and listened as the dialing began. After four rings, someone answered:

"Hello! This is Ophelia Terryman. I'm not available to take your call right now because I'm at the supermarket. But after the tone, if you'll leave a message, I'll get back to you just as soon as I can. Bye-bye!"

My heart pounded. After the bomb detonated, killing Ophelia and injuring Cody and me, the emergency people arrived and so on. Nobody had bothered to terminate the Terrymans' home phone service. I thought for a moment and pictured Vince trying to phone Ophelia that day, her landline ringing from the next room as she struggled through the door with the shoebox bomb and grocery bags. She dumped the shoebox onto the table and the bomb blew up. Had he been calling her regarding her party that evening, or to warn her of the bomb?

I crawled out of Vince's window and down the fire escape, agile as a long black cat, and returned to my vehicle. After making a brief stop at a Wendy's drive-through, I headed back out to the disaster scene in Lafayette. Once I arrived, I felt surprised, although I probably should not have, at the absence of workmen repairing house. Its front gate had been ripped away by the blast, so I just walked onto the property. This, of course, was my first visit here since New Year's Eve, and I felt much anxiety and dread at the sight of charred grass, the wreckage that had been a beautiful house, and the blackened human shape towards the front of the lawn that bore only the slightest resemblance to Ophelia Terryman.

At the front entrance, I shook my head at the smell of death and destruction I had encountered so many times as a soldier and police officer. I frowned at the boards covering the front door and the half-assed attempts at reinforcing the column that had a chunk taken out of it. The private detective in me wondered: Does Cody still live here? If so, why? Hasn't he moved in with the Normans in Sea Cliff? If he hasn't moved out of here, why not? If his house is vacant, why hasn't this disaster area been secured in any way? Where is the yellow tape? Where were the security guards? Didn't Cody or the Normans give a shit about squatters or looters?

I went into the house and left my business card by Cody's answering machine, wondering if he felt as freaked out as I did about surviving that bomb blast. To me, it was as if the Grim Reaper had pointed at me and said, *Not you, baby. Not your time yet. I'll be back for you when I'm ready.*

The traffic was moderate as I got back onto the westbound freeway and zipped across the Bay Bridge. Half an hour later I parked on the street in front of the Normans' Sea Cliff house. The sunlight made the mansion look whiter than ivory, and I looked over my shoulder to see the Bay, a magnificent azure. I heard the waves crashing against the bluffs and remembered for the hundredth time why so many people fell in love with my City by the Bay.

I saw cars parked in their circular driveway but could not tell which one belonged to whom. I knocked on the front door, the maid answered, I asked for Allison but she offered to get Edina. At that point I just wanted to speak to someone named Norman. I also wished I had something of substance to tell them. I had been running here and there for a little while now on this warehouse fire, and then there was this little matter of the Man now coming after me about that ten thousand in the bank and how I had gotten it. Hmm. So as I stood there waiting for a Norman to speak, I hoped Brynne would not appear because I had nothing to say to her, and she had nothing to say that *I* would care to hear. Not that it made hella difference which of the Normans I spoke to, but like all other men, I had my pride. Can you show me the man who wants to hang out and talk with his ex-wife's lesbian lover?

"Good afternoon, Coolidge."

Edina. She stood before me, skin smooth, body narrow, face completely inscrutable. Her face was pallid, her black T-shirt and blue jeans so tight that I wondered how she managed to breathe. Her boots added several unneeded inches to her height. I sometimes thought she looked like a poster girl for Jenny Craig, but maybe not—weight-loss clients didn't necessarily want to look anorexic. Edina, her family's wild child, craved skydiving and motorcycling, hitchhiking and picking up bad boys in roadside taverns. Maybe she was the one meant to live fast, love hard and die young, while Brynne was born to sleep long, stay stoned and do little.

"Let's talk," I said.

"Why?"

"Because your sister's dead. Brandy Capwell's dead, too."

She nodded. "Brynne mentioned that. Hard luck."

"No shit. Now, let's talk about Brynne. How did

she manage to get in on all this fun? Did you call her and ask her to fly out here?"

"Yes."

"Shame on you, bitch."

"Your own fault, Coolidge."

"Excuse me?"

"When I asked you to explain things to me, you said nothing. These are my people we're dealing with, you understand. If I ask, you answer."

"Hmm. And whose idea was it to cast Aja in this little drama?"

"Mine. But Brynne found Aja in the first place. They were lovers years ago. Brynne ended it, but they still had things to say to one another. Aja was very eager to hook up with her again, to see if they might get back together."

"Aja shouldn't have done me like that," I said.

"Well, when she came by to say, 'Hey, Cool, will you let me back into your life?' you could have said no. But you didn't, and I'm sure Aja was amazed at how easily she exploited you."

I nodded. "Yeah, it was like I pointed at my fly and said to her, 'Hit me with your best shot.' She gave you plenty of information on me."

"But we still don't know who killed my sister."

"And we still don't know who killed Brandy Capwell."

Edina sighed. "I'm very busy, Coolidge. Tell me why you're here and what you want."

"What I want," I told her, " is to know who ended up with Ophelia's stock."

"Her stock? I don't know anything about it."

"She had ten voting shares. What happened to them? She would have left them to someone in her family. Who would that be?"

Edina shrugged and blew out a big breath. "Who cares? That bomb that killed her? It was meant for Cody. He was supposed to die, not her. Isn't that right?"

"Is it right? I don't know. Who stands to gain anything by her death? You or Lloyd?"

"Allison," said the familiar voice. "The stock went to Allison."

I looked up to see Missus Norman standing on the stairs.

"Mother—"

"Coolidge, come up to my room so we can talk."

I did as told.

24

I sat in a chair and eyed her as she sat on her bed. "You what's happening around here."

"Yes. I should have told you about things sooner, but I hoped I was wrong. We all try to bury the past and pretend that the bad things did not happen, but sometimes that just isn't possible. There's so much that's regrettable and shameful in the world already." She shook her head. "I promised Guy I would never speak of these matters again."

"Talk to me, Georgia. You have to help me

understand."

"Then be quiet and listen." She took a deep breath. "We've always done our best. We tried to the right thing, and we got through the hard times with as much dignity as we could. Then we would just carry on."

"Of course you did. Don't blame yourself ."

"I *do* blame myself. I knew something was wrong but acted as though everything was fine. I'm such a fool."

"Does this have anything to do with Guy?"

"No. Lloyd."

"Lloyd?"

"It started with him. He was so rebellious, full of backtalk. He had to prove to everyone that he was his own man, that nobody could order him around. He and Guy clashed all the time."

"Allison told me that Lloyd had some problems with the law."

"He was *always* in trouble. I didn't think he was a bad son, just a confused boy who did some bad things. Lloyd seemed to look forward to living out a criminal destiny, so Guy finally said, 'Enough of this nonsense' and sent Lloyd to a military school, and then Lloyd joined the Army. We saw very little of them during those years, so when we *did* see him, we noticed the change in him. He came a man— muscular, masculine, mature. No more backtalk or poor attitudes. He told us he wanted to return to San Francisco permanently and learn his father's business. Guy was quite delighted." She sighed again and mopped her face with a hanky.

So far she had told me a bunch of shit I already knew. I hoped she would spring some new shit on me real soon. "Tell me more."

"Well, that year, Lloyd came home for a visit and things were going very well...I did quite a good job of convincing myself that Lloyd had overcome all his problems and would be a decent human being forever. It was New Year's Day and I was feeling so optimistic—but then Brynne came to us with the most outrageous story. I guess that from that day forward I've blamed her for telling me, because if she hadn't told me, I wouldn't have known, and sometimes not knowing is the best thing. Anyway, Brynne was just getting into her teens then and maybe didn't know any better than to tell. Still, she's always been full of mischief, always eager to get others in trouble."

Tell me about it. "What did Brynne say to you that got you so upset?"

"She said she'd caught Lloyd doing something awful. She tried to look very troubled by it, but I knew she was enjoying herself, telling on her brother like that and she knew how much it would disturb us."

"What," I asked her, "did Brynne catch Lloyd doing that you found so objectionable?"

She swallowed hard a couple of times and cleared her throat. "Not just Lloyd. Ophelia and Lloyd on the bed. She had just turned fourteen and was just too beautiful. I wanted to have a heart attack and die right there. Guy went batty. He was beside himself. Lloyd said, 'Brynne told you nonsense; we weren't doing anything bad.' But Guy didn't buy any of it and beat Lloyd senseless. Lloyd said, 'It happened only once and I'll never do it again.' Guy said, 'You're damn right you won't,' and he sent Ophelia away to a boarding school."

"Just you, Guy, and the two kids knew about this?"

"Plus Brynne. Nobody told Allison, but I've always had the feeling that she knew there had been some sort of tragedy in the family."

We stayed quiet for the longest time. She looked at me, then looked at the floor. A couple of times she opened her mouth, as if to say more, but then closed it and dabbed at it with her hanky.

"What else, Georgia? Tell me what else there is. I need to know."

She shook her head, wiped her eyes with her hanky and took some more deep breaths. "Lloyd was lying about it, that it was a one-time thing. He had been indecent with her many, many times. I'm grateful that Guy didn't know."

"So, you suspected that Lloyd and Ophelia were having incestuous relations but you didn't actually *do* anything about it?"

"Do *what*? I made a point of keeping them apart, which was easy enough. Lloyd always went to summer camp and Ophelia loved visiting our friends in New England. I prayed it was just a phase they were going through and that Lloyd would lose interest in his inappropriate relationship with her. I thought that maybe"—another huge sigh—"oh, Coolidge, I don't know *what* I thought! I don't know what to think now, either. I had no idea of how to broach the subject with them and I knew they would both deny it if I brought it up. Maybe it was Ophelia's idea all along."

"For how long did this 'inappropriate relationship' continue?" I asked, feeling full of contempt for the old woman but keeping my voice nice and even so she wouldn't get mad at me and end our conversation.

"As far back as I can remember. Lloyd was five when Ophelia was born, and I was afraid he would get jealous because now we had this baby that got so much of the attention that he would normally get. But he seemed to think it was wonderful that now he had this baby sister. It was just him and Edina until Ophelia was born. I don't know what motivated him to have that sort of contact with her, but it ended after they were discovered and from that point on they despised each other. Of course, those years of abuse left her with bad personal problems."

"What kind of problems? Sexual?"

"Yes. Plus severe depression and panic attacks. She ran, swam and slept—whatever it took to escape her feelings for a while. Running away from that monkey on her back. That's how she spent most of her life."

"Ophelia told me that she and Brynne had a big conflict during Thanksgiving. What do you know about that?"

She shrugged. "Oh, some sisterly nonsense. The kind of conflict you have when you've drunk too much wine. Brynne was livid at Ophelia but I suppose it was just over some ancient, petty grievance."

Another silence set in, and I thought some more about Norman Appliances, Lloyd, rumors of a takeover, evidence of insurance fraud. Someone was after Lloyd and I ended up getting caught in it. When Ophelia was killed, I had assumed it had something to do with the family business, some sort of accident. Not so. I felt the answer come to me so fast that I experienced a twinge of shame that I hadn't figured it out sooner.

I snapped my fingers. "Did Brynne tell Cody?"

She nodded. "I believe so. Cody isn't as stable as the rest of us. He has problems and he's wrapped too tightly. Even when he and Ophelia first met, he seemed a little odd and I was surprised she would marry someone like him. But he did adore her."

"'Adore'? I've heard him described as 'obsessed.'"

"I repeat: He adored her. He was just the thing she needed to boost her poor self-image. She was deeply troubled by what Lloyd had done to her and she couldn't keep a relationship going for very long. Cody seemed to give her what she needed."

"You mean that you considered her defective merchandise because of Lloyd."

"Frankly, yes. Who knows how badly Lloyd had warped her with his deviant behavior?"

"It wasn't her fault."

"I didn't say it was," Georgia retorted. "But what good man was going to make a life with her if he knew about what awful things she'd been through? I was quite happy to have Cody unaware of her past."

"So you kept quiet about the whole thing."

She nodded. "Absolutely. We swept it under the rug and acted as though it didn't exist."

"I need to make a call," I said, taking out my iPhone and dialing Lieutenant Lando's number. "Where's Cody now?" I asked the old woman.

"On his way home," she muttered, breathing hard and looking so tuckered out that I thought she might fall asleep right there.

When Lando answered the phone, I ran it all down for him.

"We'll pick him up for questioning. We'll get a search warrant so we can check out his house for evidence that he made that bomb."

"He works at a place where they build air conditioners," I said. "They would have everything he needed to build that bomb there."

"Well, let me tell you what we've come up with," Lando said. "Remember the Brandy Capwell rental car? We got a match on the prints. The owner of the prints, and therefore the guy that did her, is named Hans Enns. He got mad at his stepmother and blew her up with an explosive device not unlike the one that killed Ophelia Terryman. When Enns was tried, the jury acquitted him because of temporary insanity."

"No prison time, huh?"

"None. They put him in the state psychiatric facility but he escaped."

"Was Enns really crazy or was it just an act?"

"He blew up his stepmother because she wouldn't let him have his own way. What do *you* think?"

"Good point. Be sure to alert the Normans when you catch Enns."

"Absolutely. Must go now." Click.

I left Georgia Norman dozing in her bedroom, then found Edina and told her about my conversation in the bedroom. As I headed for the front door, Edina hurried upstairs, presumably to speak to her mother, and I couldn't begin to imagine what they would say to each other. I drove home feeling exhausted and frustrated. Sometimes I get fed up with confronting people and listening as they tell me things that are none of my business. Lloyd Norman was screwing his sister? Yuck. Why can't they go back into the past and remember the good things? No wonder shrinks are booked up for eternity; so many people have so much bad shit they need to talk about to a professional stranger.

I soon reached the Tenderloin and, as usual, marveled at the spectacular wealth I had recently left and the grinding poverty that was home, sweet home. I parked my car, promised to buy myself a new one when I could afford to do so. I entered the lobby and checked my mail, picturing Aja and Brynne in a naked embrace and then pushing them apart as I entered the elevator. Back in my microloft, I dropped my knapsack on the floor and felt like taking a shower that I scarcely needed. I wanted to scrub off all that sordid shit Georgia Norman had dumped all over me. I would get all prettied up, then walk over to Orlanda's and knock on her door till she let me in and gave me dinner. She was due back from holidays by now, and although it was just past four, maybe she would let me in early. I wanted a large, fattening meal with beer and dessert, and I wanted Orlanda to talk my ear off.

I took off my jacket and looked at my bathroom door. The door was closed. For my own neurotic little reasons, I'd always kept it open when not using it; why was it closed now? I could practically hear someone breathing behind that door. My heart pounded, my pulse raced, much as it had when I was a cop and knew that serious danger lay behind this door or around that corner. Then I watched as the knob turned and the door swung open. I saw the gun first, pointed at my chest. I raised my hands.

"Coolidge," muttered Cody. "I wasn't expecting you just yet. Thought I had plenty of time to make my getaway."

"What do you want?"

"Just came by to give you a little something. Look in the kitchen cupboard."

I did as he said and found another shoebox wrapped in paper. I felt more hungry than scared. Famished and terrified. A bad combination.

"Did you make this yourself?" I asked him.

"With a little help from the tools at Norman Appliances," he said. "Open it."

"I think I'll just stand here and admire it."

"Don't worry if you drop it. It's got a timer, you see."

I was pretty sure my gun was in my knapsack. Nice place for it. I looked at the shoebox, considered its destructive capacity, thought of the man standing a few feet away, who had killed his wife, was trying to kill me and probably had a few other victims in mind.

"Well," I told him, "if this mofo is gonna blow, maybe you oughta git."

"Oh, I can hang with you for a few minutes."

"What up with this? Why off me?"

"Why not?"

"You gonna git Lloyd?"

"He's next."

"Mind if I sit down?" I asked.

"It's your place." He looked around. "Damn, this place ain't big enough for Danny DeVito."

"Well, Danny don't come around much." I pulled up one of my chairs and sat. Cody pulled up the other one. He was a big dude and, up till now, seemed like a decent enough guy. He wasn't crazy; he, like Aja, was sociopathic, and sociopaths often were as bad as crazies. Worse.

I sat and looked around. Normally I felt safe in my

puny place. It wasn't even dark yet. I needed to piss, bad. I also became aware of a deuce or two that required dropping.

"So, Cody, how much longer do I have?"

"About ten minutes, maybe twelve. I worried that you wouldn't get here on time. I know how brutal the traffic is in San Francisco. I could reset the bomb's timer, but why bother?"

"You seem nice and comfy, sittin' there and chillin'," I told him.

"Hey, I feel terrific. *I'm* not the one that's gonna be blown all over Turk Street in a few minutes."

I felt I needed to keep him talking. Maybe I expected Lando and his boys to burst in at any moment and save me. I don't know *what* the fuck I felt. I just new I felt like shit.

"What if it went off right now?" I asked. "We would both be fucked."

He shrugged. "Gotta go sometime. This life sucks anyway."

"Since this is probably the last conversation I'm ever going to have, I want you to tell me about Huey Capwell."

"Do you know about a huge government contract Norman Appliances was going to bid on?"

I nodded. "Air conditioners for the Army."

"Yes. Well, since it was a big military thing, we needed government clearances, fingerprints and all that shit. So Guy made Huey the security officer for it—you know, the guy in charge of all the applications and documents. Huey, man, you might have thought he was the director of the fuckin' CIA, the way he was digging into everyone's past."

"Including yours."

"Yeah, and I had some serious shit in my past that I was *not* eager to have Huey Capwell or anyone else know about."

"Like your stepmother."

"Yessir."

"I'm surprised that you've been free for this long. In this computer age, with DNA markers and other high-tech shit, it's easy enough to track people down."

He nodded. "Too easy, especially when you've got elephants to hide like I do."

"Did Brandy Capwell have to die?" I asked.

"Damn straight. You had to fly out to Chicago like a dumbass and connected with Brandy. Then she called *me* and said, 'I've got some information Huey had about some bad guy named Hanns Enns.' So she flew out here and I offed her."

"Ophelia loved you. Are you sorry you killed her?"

"She was profoundly unhappy. She's gone off to a better place."

"I suppose you get a great deal of comfort from that thought." I looked at the clock and saw that we had about five minutes left.

"How did you get Vince Stanich to help?"

Cody shrugged. "Gave him some money and told him that if he didn't cooperate with me I would make his life a living hell. He and I had known each other for years, and I knew what a wuss he was. Some guys are just way too easy to push around."

"Have you killed him yet?"

"Nope, he got away before I could. I'm not worried. I'll catch up with him. He's thick as a brick."

"That bomb you used to kill Ophelia? You almost got me, too."

He nodded. "Too bad I didn't. It would have saved me this trip."

I looked down on the floor, remembering that my Glock was in my knapsack. "Cody," I said, "I have a headache this big"—I held my hands two feet apart—"and it's got Tylenol written all over it. All right if I get some out of my bag?"

"No," he said, snarling. "Leave it there."

I reached down anyway and unzipped my knapsack.

"Didn't you hear me? I said to leave it alone!"

I could feel the cool polymer handle of my gun as I wrapped my fingers around it. I clicked off the safety and pointed the weapon in Cody's general direction. Then I fired.

He jumped up out of his seat, as I knew he would, but he didn't fall flat on his face, as I had hoped. Instead, he threw himself at me as I tried to pull the gun out of the knapsack. He threw a punch which landed on the side of my head and hurt like a motherfucker. I got to my feet, holding onto the wall so I wouldn't end up on my knees. I couldn't figure out where my Glock had run off to, but Cody stood there, aiming his piece at me. I grabbed my knapsack and swung it at him, catching him flush in the face. He slammed against the far wall but maintained a solid grip on his weapon.

I knew my door was locked and I would not have enough time to unlock it and run down the hallway before he fired at me, so I darted past him and threw myself into the bathroom. I locked the door and crouched as he fired twice, the bullets zinging over my head, missing me by inches. I looked around my bathroom and saw that the only thing I had to defend myself with was myself. He started kicking in the door, his big foot shattering the flimsy material as an axe would chop through old wood. To catch him by surprise, I threw open the door and slammed my own foot into his stuff. He screamed in pain and doubled over, one hand cupped over his jewels, the other still brandishing his handgun. He tried to kick at me some more but his attempts were lame. It is difficult to kick when one is experiencing testicular trauma.

I watched him fall then, his face white and contorted in agony. By then his clothing had become soaked with blood. I had hit him after all, but he taken this long to collapse. He struggled for breath and I could hear the ticking of the bomb. It would go at any moment. I leaped over Cody and grabbed the shoebox, grateful that I was strong and quick and that my window overlooking Turk Street was just a couple of steps away. I heaved the deadly package through the closed window and grimaced at the sound of busted glass. But my strength was adequate and the shoebox flew in a neat arc over the street when it exploded, well above the traffic hurrying past my building. A blinding flash of orange light and a deafening roar filled the Tenderloin. I was blown backwards and tripped over Cody's prostrate body. The bomb's impact wore off soon enough—I guessed it looked and sounded worse than it was— but I assumed it had blown out some of my neighbors' windows and maybe caused damage to the exterior of our building.

I sat up against my wall for the longest time, telling myself to find my iPhone and call the cops. But then I heard the sirens' blare, so I just sat there and stared at Cody Terryman's dead body.

IT'S ALL GOOD

EPILOGUE

Emma Hendrix returned from Philadelphia to discover that many of the building's windows had been blown to nothing. However, she showed more concern over my difficult holiday season than about what Cody Terryman's bomb had done to the property she managed. She didn't have to worry; my injuries healed up and I went back to work at Mutual of Northern California. Lowell Mitchell had my office fixed up as his way of saying sorry, and Vince Stanich lost his job and had to face criminal charges.

I contacted Lando about the ten thousand dollars Cody had deposited it into my account. Lando said, "Keep it," and I said, "Thanks, I'll do that."

IT'S ALL GOOD

www.ingramcontent.com/pod-product-compliance
Lightning Source LLC
Chambersburg PA
CBHW030327130626
46554CB00011B/269